MW01490926

∞

CUTTING TEETH

by

K.J. STEVENS

11/12

Published by Crooked Steeple Press

First Edition 2012

Manufactured in the United States of America.

ISBN: 978-1-105-63891-6

Cover art by Rita L. Stevens

∞

~ For Brooke ~

BOOKS BY K.J. STEVENS

A Better Place
Infidelity
Dead Bunnies
Landscaping
Pilgrim's Bay

THE FICTION
short stories

THE REALITY
journal entries from 2010 to 2012

January, 1932

"Eschew the monumental. Shun the Epic. All the guys who can paint great big pictures can paint great small ones."

~ Ernest Hemingway

THE FICTION

an introduction

Not long ago, I proposed this idea—CUTTING TEETH—to a literary agent in ANY CITY, U.S.A.

"You need to develop a platform," she said.

Platform? I thought. *I just want to write.*

"You need to choose. Fiction or nonfiction. It cannot be both."

Why not? I thought.

"Book marketing is a tough business," she said. "If you can't decide what it is you're writing then you can't expect people to want to read it."

My gut reaction was to tell her to go to hell.

But because I am getting older and more patient—and because she was a friend of a friend—I figured it was best to keep my mouth shut. And so, for a few weeks, I thought about what she said. Considered it. Even produced a draft copy of CUTTING TEETH that included only *THE REALITY*.

"What happened to *THE FICTION?*" S.B. said to me one night.

We had just settled into the couch. She was reading the draft copy of the book. I was reading *The Alpena News.* We were drinking wine.

"I took that agent's advice and removed the short stories," I said.

She set the book on her lap. Sipped her Merlot. Turned on the television.

"That's bullshit," she said.

I put down the paper. Looked at her.

"What did you say?"

"'Bullshit,' that's what I said. You're going to let some woman you've never met, that doesn't know you, tell you how to put together your book?"

"Honey, she's a literary agent. She knows about publishing, marketing, selling …"

S.B. held up her hand. Stopped my words in mid-air.

"But what does she know about writing?"

"She knows how to sell it. How to market it," I said.

She moved through channels. Sipped wine.

"Since when did you start caring about selling your writing?"

I folded the paper. Got up and set it in the basket next to the fireplace. Stretched and yawned.

"I don't care about selling," I said. "I just want to write."

"Then do it," she said. "Just do it the way you want to do it. Who cares what some literary agent says?"

I sat down. Sipped wine. Said nothing else about it. But for days I kept picking up that draft copy and thinking the same thing.

It IS bullshit. I've never cared about selling. All I've ever wanted to do was write and share it. Fuck it, I'm putting the stories back in.

And so, I did.

My wife—she knows me. She understands what it is I'm aiming for. And it is something that cannot be categorized, pigeon-holed, made up nice to fit into one section at a book store.

I'm a year shy of 40 and have been writing for 20 years. If I had given a shit about selling or what agents, publishers—what anybody thinks about my writing—I would have stopped long ago. Caring so much about what others think is paralyzing. Stifling. The quickest way to not writing worth a damn or not writing at all. And because all I have ever known is that I am meant to be here writing, that is exactly what I do. Little by little. A few paragraphs at a time. Words strung together during moments stolen from the everyday. Until we get here.

The end.

Which is, of course, the beginning of another book. One that will not sell. One that will not be widely read. But one that is mine. And one that is yours. Fiction *and* nonfiction together in one book, but all of them stories just the same. Simple stories. Just the way it should be.

So thank you Literary Agent in ANY CITY, U.S.A.

And thank *you*, S.B.

This one's for you.

~ K.J.

man's struggle

1.

Warm blue sky. White sun. Dad's driving. I'm riding shotgun. It is my eighteenth birthday. To celebrate, Dad's taking me fishing. On a sixty mile round trip. Out of Maple Ridge and up US 23 North. Past Long Lake and Grand Lake. Away from Pilgrim's Bay and into Knee High Harbor where we turn right off the pavement onto Split Forest Road. An old logging trail that's been dozed and filled, dozed and filled, but rises and sags year after year. There are deep trenches and potholes. Buried logs and big rocks. There are stretches of loose gravel and sand. It takes a sturdy four-wheel-drive and an experienced driver to navigate this road. Dad does it one-handed and smiling while the old F-150 shakes to pieces.

All along Split Forest Road there are grassy two-tracks. Places, Dad says, used by downstaters that call themselves hunters for two weeks out of the year. And so, every November, these men—from cities like Farmington Hills, Royal Oak, and West Bloomfield—park their shiny pickups, gadget-filled SUVs, and travel trailers in our woods to make it their own. They fasten heavy duty tarps from tree to tree with rope, bungees, and nails. They dig holes for fire pits. Put out tables and chairs. And they eat and drink and shit and piss and kill in our woods. All within a mile of Split Forest Road. The downstaters never travel far down the two-tracks. They are a different breed, Dad says. They refuse to go deep to where boots must be watertight, there is no cell phone reception, and a man must not be afraid of being alone. The good thing, Dad says, is that theirs is a destruction that comes but once a year. They are the weak hunting the weak, and the deer they kill are deer that will not last anyway. And for the most part, the downstaters take out of the woods what they've brought in. Except for bits of knotted rope, shreds of blue tarp, and nails. Some of it in, around, and hanging from trees as the F-150 rattles us down the road.

The two-tracks are used by locals too, Dad says. But these men—from The Ridge, Pilgrim's Bay, and Knee High—men that live and breathe these woods—will follow a two-track to its end. They hunt in pairs or alone. Deep in the swamp or high up on the hardwood ridge. They tuck themselves into makeshift blinds. Perch in trees. Crouch behind stumps and deadfalls. They sit on old milk crates at the edges of fields. And they wait because they know that waiting is the most important part. These men know the bedding areas, the natural shooting lanes, and when the deer come and go. They hunt by wind, the gut, and the good common sense that is learned only by the accrual of patience that comes from trial-and-error. They use hand-me-down rifles that fit them like gloves. They aim steady. Follow through. Make clean kills and drag dead bucks for miles through swamp and woods with nothing but the natural power God gave them.

"Shot Cliffy back there," Dad says, as we pass a two-track.

Cliffy is buck number three. A nine-point skull mount bolted to a rafter in our garage between Billy and Dicky. Just one in a long line of twenty-six that Dad has named alphabetically.

"Scouted him a whole year before I got him."

I've heard this a dozen times, yet it amazes me. Bucks Archie through Zero—none smaller than 160 lbs and eight points—were the result of hard work and dedication. Dad did not use doe-in-heat scent or buck calls. He did not hunt over feed piles or salt blocks. He took to the woods like a writer to words. A painter to canvas. A surgeon to muscle and bone. With patience, good judgment, and passion.

"Why don't you hunt anymore?"

Dad scans the road, the woods, the sky. Looks around as if it's the first time he's seen trees, sky, sunshine.

"There aren't any more letters in the alphabet."

"Come on, you didn't stop just because you ran out of letters."

Dad chuckles.

"No, maybe not."

"Then what? Why did you stop hunting?"

"Don't feel like killing, I guess."

"But you could scout them and shoot pictures instead."

Dad smiles and nods.

"I wish your Mom would have let me take you hunting when you were a kid."

"We could try this fall."

"It's too late, Will. A man has to hunt in his early days, otherwise it doesn't stick."

"What doesn't stick?"

"It's hard to explain, but when hunting is done right, it's something you grow out of."

"But you like venison."

"I love venison sausage and jerky."

"And Mom's venison stew," I remind him.

"And Mom's venison stew," he says.

Each of us leaves to daydream. I'm not sure where Dad goes, but I am gone away to an old December. Christmas Eve morning. Mom is in the living room at the woodstove. Wearing red flannel pajamas. Stirring a wooden spoon inside our big, cast iron pot. The Christmas tree glows. Big, white flakes swirl outside the window. Bing Crosby sings *Silent Night* and Mom hums along. The smells of venison and steak spice, brown peppery gravy and vegetables tease my nose. And even though my brain leads me to the kitchen for Apple Jacks, my stomach rumbles hard for the stew. But it is too early for something so heavy and lasting, and it is not meant to be eaten until later that evening. After each of us has opened one present and we are gathered together, cozy by the fire, watching *It's a Wonderful Life* on the tube.

The old Ford hammers a hole so hard that the shocks and springs bottom out and the frame scrapes a high spot in the road. It's a real kidney shaker. Snaps me from my daydream. But Dad is still gone away. Reliving a good day in the past or imagining better days to come. A big happy smile hangs from cheek to cheek.

My stomach grumbles.

"We don't have venison much anymore," I say.

"No, but we have beef and pork and chicken, and for those there's always someone else willing to do the killing."

I think of steaks and chops wrapped in foam and cellophane. Fruits and vegetables all waxy and shimmering under grocery store sprinklers and fluorescent lights. We never really know where the food comes from. It does not look like big-eyed cows and chubby pink pigs. It does not look like feathers and beaks. It does not look like hunch-backed migrant workers with gnarled fingers. It does not look like sun-leathered skin or calloused hands. And it does not smell like slaughterhouses or processing plants. It only looks and smells and tastes like food that is fit for pots, pans, and plates.

We pass more two-tracks. Flowers are blooming. Grass and trees greening. But there are other things too. Broken chairs and stained mattresses. Bulging, black garbage bags. Gutted couches. Old washing machines.

"Why do people do that?"

"Do what?" Dad asks.

"Throw garbage into the woods."

His smile falls away.

"Son, most men cut ties and hide their mistakes instead of sack up and be men. This stuff here—the old furniture, rusting appliances, and garbage—that's our world today. The pussification of the American Male. Men tossing aside and hiding things that they don't know how to handle. Their wives. Their kids. Their garbage. And for that, the woods is a perfect place for hiding."

Dad points ahead to the steep hill in the road. Near the top, there is a deer. Standing broadside, watching us. We have seen hundreds of deer. On drives through the countryside. In the woods behind our house. And in the mornings and evenings nearly every day, as they make their way from bedding areas to feeding areas and back again. For a long time, Dad carried a pencil and a spiral bound notebook under the seat of the truck. DEER LOG was written across the front cover, and for years he kept records.

October 23, 1990 – 4 deer total.
Kowalski's field:
8:50 am. About 35 degrees. Slight frost on ground. Clear sky.
Three does with darker than usual fur.
One six-point buck with a thick neck. Sniffing around them like crazy.
Early rut and a heavy winter coming.

Pages and pages of locations, times, weather conditions, and observations. Some of them in his handwriting. A few in mine. But most of them in Mom's. She was his calendar. Binoculars. His weathervane. The one that tied it all together. His pencil to the paper that faithfully capturing everything.

March 6, 1995 – not a deer in sight. It is 1:15 pm. We've been driving for over an hour. Around the same back roads. Over and over and over again. I cannot count how many times we've done this. I'm not sure why we do this. But I love you—my big, deer-loving husband, and I will continue to sit here and look out windows and count deer and check my watch and validate your guesses at temperature, even when you are grumpy because you've had too many beers the night before.

Dad *was* grumpy a lot. Especially in my younger years. It could have been the drinking. Maybe it was the recurring bouts of unemployment. Mostly, I think it was because he had believed that he was meant for bigger things. He had dreams. But life—marriage, raising a boy, making ends meet—broke him down and fit him into a much smaller world. He got older. Sobered up. And settled into a full time union job at the steel mill. He grew patient. Calm. And he became a quiet man. He was passionate about reading, hunting, fishing, and family. He was master of his emotions. Had steady hands. And carried himself as a humble, strong man.

And so, as we approach the deer on the hill, it is worrisome to me to see Dad's hand shaking as he reaches under the seat and feels around for the DEER LOG that's not been there for years.

"Aw, shit ..." Dad says.

"What?" I ask.

"Nothing," he says.

He is embarrassed. Frustrated. Disappointed. Reaching for something that's gone.

Dad points at the deer as it turns to face us. It is young. Likely a doe. And there is an arrow—a few inches of it, anyway—sticking out from her flank. The deer walks toward us. We drive toward it. We say nothing. She turns broadside, then stands still enough to show us her mark—the red-white-and-blue plastic arrow flights that she wears against her brown fur.

"We're a virus," Dad says. "A goddamned virus that's infected the earth."

Dad says this without anger, but under those words and his calm demeanor there is *something*. A depth. A lifetime of thought and experience that has got him to this opinion. He has within him the culmination of moments and days. Good and bad. It is silent and steady on the surface, but only because over the years he has learned a few sensible things. Talk little. Listen lots. Challenge yourself to be better. To be strong. Physically, mentally, and spiritually. Trust the gut. Take a punch before giving one. And always, do the best you can. Simple, common sense. Things that everyone knows, but for some reason, cannot exercise.

"A goddamned virus," he says once more.

There is nothing to say to this, and as I watch the deer walk away into the woods—her badge of courage glinting as it catches a sun ray—I believe what Dad says is true.

We approach the bottom of the hill and Dad locks the truck into creeper gear. We chug our way up. Slowly. Deliberately. And I imagine that this is what it must be like in a rollercoaster as it clinks and pulls its way to the top of a great fall. Stones shift and pop beneath the heavy tread. The tired chassis twists and squeaks. The motor grumbles. Dust rises through rusty holes in the floor and the doors and fills the cab so that I can taste it—the sand, the dirt, the crust of the earth—and as I stare out at the green swampy ditches filled with standing water, cattails and tall grass, I can't help but feel that something is watching. And patient. And waiting to swallow us whole.

2.

I am old enough to vote. To die for my country. To buy cigarettes and porn. Still, if Mom was alive, she'd fuss about this trip. It wouldn't matter that I've grown. That I'm making the trip with Dad. To her, this was no place for a boy let alone a man. Split Forest Road—like a lot of places she'd never been—had a sinister hold on her that I could never understand. Mom was like that about a lot of things. Gutsy and honest, but stubborn and fearful, she had opinions and thoughts, reasons and ways that could never fully be explained. She lived by heart and feeling. I loved her honestly and truly, but most days my natural affection for her was shackled and beaten by sheer frustration. She believed in God, but didn't go to church. She cooked and sewed and cleaned and took pride in the fact that she was a housewife, but she believed that people should be able to support themselves. She never wanted to be more, see more, hear more, or know more, but she always asked questions and was a bit of a gossip. She knew a lot about a few things— gardening, canning, cooking, cleaning, and family—but by the way she talked and acted, she clearly thought she knew everything. She'd grown up in Pilgrim's Bay and had never left. She went to Mackinaw Island once when she was in sixth grade. She liked the horses there, she said. And the buildings and the fudge, but she'd never go again. The ferry ride made her sick. And when crossing the Mackinac Bridge, she was sure it would collapse and she would die.

"The boat ride was loud and cold. The waves nearly knocked us over! And that bridge? It's unnatural to have concrete and steel spanning open water like that! Water is meant for drinking and washing. Not crossing."

Mom lived by Dorothy's mantra in *The Wizard of Oz*. There is, and was, no place like home. Everything we needed was right in our own backyard. And because of that, I wasn't allowed to go anywhere.

I couldn't stay the night at Stevie Weckmeyer's because Mrs. Weckmeyer didn't keep a clean house and Mr. Weckmeyer was a drunk.

"You'll catch a staph infection or come home craving rum ice cream. There's no way any child of mine is staying at that dump!"

I couldn't ride bikes with Jimmy Dilworth because his parents spoiled him rotten and let him do whatever he wanted.

"That's all I need. You coming back all high-and-mighty after roaming the countryside all day. There's no way any child of mine is going to be spoiled rotten then come home thinking he's ruler of the roost!"

I didn't get to join after school activities, play sports, or take part in field trips. And I didn't even mention it when Maple Ridge School asked us to sell candy bars to earn a trip to Mackinac Island. My chances of crossing the bridge or bouncing along the big lake in a ferry boat were about as good as my chances of going to the moon. I sold the candy bars anyway, but only one box and all of them to Dad. He bought fifty chocolate caramel bars and stashed them in the garage. It was our little secret. A treat we shared every time something fun came along and Mom shot it down.

"Mom, the Smith twins are having a birthday party at Maggie's Pizza this Saturday and ..."

"Maggie's Pizza? I don't think so. Your Aunt Cindy got food poisoning there and hasn't been right since. And when did you get so chummy with the Smith twins? Didn't they steal your marbles?"

So, into the garage with Dad I went. We sat, commiserated, and ate candy bars.

"Mom, they want me to try out for the part of Tiny Tim for the school play. I think I've got a chance of getting the part, but ... "

"Tiny Tim? You're bigger than every boy in your class! Is it a satire? A spoof? Sounds fishy to me. Schools nowadays with their liberal educating and sports and plays and music. You're at school to learn! I guess it's high time I call Principal Peters and give him a piece of my mind."

And so it went. Dad and I eating candy bar after candy bar until they were gone and when they ran out we bought hard candies and taffy from Mann's Corner Store. Every time he heard the broken-wing flight of another of my ideas shot to the ground, he asked me to help in the garage. And there we would sit. Listening to country oldies on WATZ. Crinkling wrappers. Crunching candy. Savoring the bitter sweetness that only defeat could bring.

3.

In those days, my only saving grace and constant source of pleasure was Sheila Carmichael. The fifteen-year-old girl that moved in next door when I was thirteen. She was sweet and sassy, of little words, and what endeared her most to me was her ability to push Mom's buttons. Sheila was never outright disrespectful. Never rude. She was, like me, just a dumb teenager. An awkward body coursing with hormones. A head full of big ideas without plans.

"She's a slut in the making!" Mom said, "Prancing around half-naked all the time. If that was *my* daughter I'd have nipped that in the bud a long time ago!"

But Sheila wasn't half naked *all* the time. That started the year she turned sixteen. When she'd been blessed, almost overnight, with the body of a twenty year old. It was awe-inspiring the way she ran through our lawn sprinklers on hot summer days. Stringiest of string bikinis. Tight bronze skin glistening in the mist. A sight so raw and untamed that it rifled through my gut and shot vibrations through muscle, tissue, bone. Made me feel there was nothing else in the world. Just me. The sprinklers. The thick wet grass. And Sheila Carmichael. Shimmering liquid diamonds in the summer sun.

But of course, it was never only Sheila and I. Always, there in the background, was Mom.

"This isn't the damned water park, missy!"

Red-faced and sweating mad. Reeking of cucumbers, vinegar, and dill because she'd been canning all day, Mom stormed out of the house to confront Sheila.

"Sorry, Miss Jenkins," Sheila said. "I was just coolin' off is all."

"Well, cool off at home! You have water there don't you?"

Shelia smiled, "The water's better over here."

Mom shut off the hose and grabbed my arm.

"And you, Mr. Beach Boy! Into the house and into the shower. Ice cold!"

From that day forward, the sprinklers ran only at night. And I was left waiting. Counting the seconds until 9:45 when the sweet sound of water against aluminum siding sent lightning through my veins and I was alone. Thinking long and hard about Sheila Carmichael. Bronze and wet. Bounding through the mist. Mine again.

There were other incidents that contributed to the end of my infatuation with Sheila. Like the Saturday morning she came over for cereal and cartoons. When Mom answered the door and Sheila, in all her bright-eyed morning glory, stood there wearing only a tight pink tank top and itty-bitty sleeping shorts. Clutching a box of Apple Jacks to her chest.

"If it's all right, Willy and I are going to eat a little cereal and watch Looney Tunes."

Mom took the box.

"There's no *Willy* here. If you're referring to *William*, my son, he's already had breakfast, and both of you are too old for cartoons."

Mom slammed the door. Went to the kitchen. Got a bowl, a spoon, the milk, and poured herself some Apple Jacks. I watched Sheila through the living room curtains as she stopped in our yard, bent over, picked a dandelion and put it in her hair. She stood a moment—smiling at the big warm sky—then yawned and stretched a long satisfying stretch and shivered when she was done. She took a few long, easy strides then skipped home. I sighed and ached. Sought distraction in Bugs Bunny and his pals.

Then, late one summer day, while washing Mom's car, Sheila came over to help. I knew that this was a bad idea. That it would not end well, but my gut was warm and my heart skipping beats and I knew it would do no good to tell her to leave. By now, Sheila knew that Mom hated her. That she was not welcome in or around our home, but this did not deter her. Mom's hatred drove Sheila to say what she said, do what she did, and wear what she wore. And on this day, God bless her, she was wearing a sheer, snug white t-shirt and a little black skirt. It was an incredible sight. Something I could have never imagined, but was happy to see because I knew I could return to it over and over again when I was lonely.

It was when Sheila was bent over, putting her whole body into a generous scrubbing of the whitewalls, that I noticed there wasn't anything under that skirt. And it was at that exact moment that Mom burst out of the house with a frying pan held high above her head, howling and screaming mad. Dad ran out after her, and I was frozen in my tracks, holding the bucket and the hose, caught somewhere between a boner and dumbfounded terror. The action unfolded quickly, in a rush, but what I remember most was Sheila all wet and soapy, her small dark nipples pushing through her shirt, Mom swinging that pan and Dad's big hand coming round to snatch it away just before it hit Sheila's head. He threw Mom over his shoulder, tossed the frying pan to the ground, and carried Mom into the house as she yelled.

"LEAVE MY FAMILY ALONE!"

Sheila, for the first time ever, looked scared.

"What was *that* all about?" Sheila asked.

"Supper must be ready," I said, and I picked up the frying pan and went into the house.

With all the fuss, Mom pushing Sheila away and Sheila still coming around, it was no wonder that our relationship ended the way it did. One week after the car washing incident. Sheila topless and belly down on our family picnic table. Me over top of her, wearing nothing but a pair of swim trunks, working tanning lotion into her glorious skin. She was pulling down her bikini bottom just a hitch so I could cover every inch when Mom raced into the yard.

"What in the hell's going on?" she hollered.

"Aw, nothin', Miss Jenkins. Willy was just helpin' me prevent sunburn is all."

"Sunburn? Well if that isn't the biggest bunch of bullshit … Get off my picnic table and off my property this instant! I don't want to see you in my yard or near my boy ever again!"

Sheila rose slowly. Her small, smooth breasts were firm and tight and I could not take my eyes off them as she yawned and then stretched like a cat waking from a nap. She picked her bikini top up from the table and handed it to me. She kissed my cheek. Tussled my hair. Picked my Dukes of Hazzard t-shirt from the ground and put it on.

"Perfect fit," she said.

Mom was flabbergasted. Shocked. Could not manage a word.

Sheila smiled at her, winked, and blew her a kiss.

I was amazed. Awed. In love. It looked as if Sheila Carmichael— the neighborhood tramp—had gotten the last word.

We stood silently and watched as Sheila walked—barefoot and carefree—across our lawn. She picked two daisies. Tucked one over each ear, then danced one last time through sprinklers that weren't even turned on.

"She's on her way to being a pogo stick junkie," Mom hissed. "And by God, I'm going to put a stop to it."

She pointed to the house. I bowed my head, guts whirling with excitement and dread, and I walked inside.

Later that night, alone in my room with thoughts of Sheila thrumming my veins, I heard Mom on the phone with Sheila's Dad.

A man she'd never met before. A person she did not know. And yet, she called him a drunk, a pothead, and even questioned his sexuality. She said he provided no fatherly guidance. Told him that the world was doomed if it depended on men like him to raise and provide for the next generation. I was furious. Hurt. Embarrassed for him. I wanted to run out of my room, into the kitchen, grab the phone from her and yank the wires from the wall. But it was unnecessary. No use. Too late. The damage had been done.

"Well, good night and screw you too, Mr. Carmichael!"

Only she didn't say screw, if you know what I mean.

Mom hung up the phone. Let out a little growl. Then walked down the hallway to my room. She knocked and came in. I reached over and turned on the light. Expected an earful.

"Well, that takes care of that," she said.

I said nothing.

"Do you need anything before I go to bed?"

Still, I said nothing.

"Anything at all?" she asked.

Mom's bright green eyes locked onto mine. She opened her mouth to speak, but no words came. We stared and stared. At each other. Into each other. And I began to burn with all the things she'd ever done to make me sad, or mad, feel unworthy and dumb. And then, I said something I could never take back.

"Why are you always such a bitch?"

Tears started down her cheeks. Silence grew heavy between us. I did not think of her as the woman that carried me inside of her for nine months. I did not think of her as the woman that bathed me, changed me, fed me, and kept me warm. I could only think of her as the obstacle between me and the rest of my life. The friends I would not have, the girls I would not kiss, and the life I would not live because my mother would not let go.

She broke her eyes from mine. Wiped her tears.

"I'm sorry," she said. "You just don't understand. All of this— what I do—it's out of love. "

I turned out the light.

"William?"

I said nothing and buried my head under the pillow.

"Willy?"

I felt her come near. Stand over me. But I didn't move.

"You can't see it now, but one day you will," she said. "This world is a bad place and I'm doing all I can to protect you."

"Go away."

"You'll see, Willy. One day, something will happen—something horrible—and you will feel your world breaking in two. And then you will see. You'll see like me and you'll realize that there is black and there is white. There is right and there is wrong. And until you reach that day, you cannot understand."

"Go away, I said."

She waited there a few seconds, then left. She closed the door, walked down the hallway, and busied herself like she always did, cleaning well into the night. I sat and stared out the window at moonlight on the dewy grass and felt an uneasy change taking shape. It was unsettling. Fierce. So strange to me that I wanted to pack my bags, hop on my bike, and ride away from my room, my house, and my family for good.

Later, I woke to the sounds of Mom sniffling and crying in the kitchen. Dad was there with her. Not saying much, only shifting in his chair once in a while and pulling tissues from the box. I felt no regret or guilt for what I had done and as I gazed into the big night sky, I realized that things between us would never be the same.

4.

We crest the hill. Gain speed. And coast into a rough stretch of washboard bumps. The truck shakes and bounces until it is moving sideways in the road. Dad pumps the brakes and wrestles the steering wheel. When we stop, we are inches from the ditch.

"Your Mom lost an uncle back here," he says, and pops the truck out of creeper gear.

"Did he get shaken to death?" I ask.

Dad laughs, backs up the truck, straightens us out, and gets us moving again.

"No, son. The bears got him. And that is probably the biggest reason Mom wouldn't let you back here."

The truck wheels over one last back-breaking trench and finally the road levels out.

"How'd the bears get him?"

"He was fishing alone and got caught up in the swamp muck. The *quicksand*, as your mother called it. It's awfully deep in places and sometimes when you step in you can't step out. Poor guy was a meatball stuck in gravy to those bears. All they found was a boot. Part of a leg. Fishing gear and bloody shreds."

Dad nods toward the bed of the truck.

"That spear back there, the one I use, that was his."

I take a minute to digest this. Peer into the tall grass, the thick swamp, and wonder what it's like to even see a bear.

"It didn't help that he was a drunk," Dad says. "And fishing near a marsh during cub season. I bet he was three sheets to the wind when all of it happened. If he'd been sober, he might have come out alive."

Dad stops the truck on a small bridge. We get out, lean on the railing and look at the water. It is not as I had expected. It is only a foot wide, a few inches deep, and barely moving. I look to Dad. He is gazing at a muddy clump of weeds, branches and trees piled high in the middle of the creek. A large beaver is in the water, dragging a sapling toward the heap.

"I'll be damned," Dad says, and winks.

He moves the truck. Parks it on one of the two-tracks. This one has no garbage. Only tall grass and a few empty beer cans. We pick them up, toss them into the back of the truck and grab our buckets and spears. We walk down a narrow path from the road, through the ditch, and into thick brush. The sun beams. Heat rises. And the smell of dead fish hangs on the breeze as we push through thorny berry bushes. The ground is soft and sucks at our boots as we carry our gear to the water. I think of Mom's drunk uncle stumbling through the swamp all those years ago and wonder if what Dad's said is true. Maybe we are a virus. The human race. And maybe God or Mother Nature sends in the bears every once in a while to do some cleaning. But I suspect it is bigger than me and bigger than Dad. Bigger than swamps and creeks and two-tracks. And it is too much to think about on my eighteenth birthday when all I want to do is spear suckers so that we can take them home, gut them, clean them, and prepare them for smoking.

"Be careful," Dad says, as he points to a patch of ground he has maneuvered around. But it is too late. My feet have found the spot. The black muck has taken hold. And I am sinking past my knees. It happens so quickly that I'm dazed and confused and it isn't until I'm up to my crotch that I realize Mom's quicksand has got me. Dad reaches out with his spear handle. It is worn and gouged. Dark spots stain the wood. And as I grab hold, I wonder if the marks are from bear claws, a man's struggle, his blood.

"Hold tight!" Dad shouts. Veins bulge and throb in his neck and forearms. The wet earth wants to keep me, make me its own, but it cannot. Dad gives a great tug. And when I'm out, we smile and breathe deep and he pats me on the back. We watch as the black hole collapses into itself and takes my boot and sock away.

"I could've been a goner."

Dad stares at the spear in his hand.

"Just think," he said, "If your Mom's uncle hadn't got killed, I wouldn't have had this spear."

We manage to laugh it off and then waste no time getting barefoot and into the water. We spear the few dead suckers that are stuck in the beaver dam and fling them onto the shore. Seagulls call from high above then swoop down to land. They pick and tear and swallow. Cry with full bellies to the brilliant sky.

Once we've cleared the dead, we set to work breaking the dam. It's hard and messy work, but it's work that needs to be done so that the water and the suckers are free again.

"We need to move these logs," Dad says.

We throw our spears onto the shore. Remove sticks and logs by hand.

"Some of these look like they've been cut with a saw," I say.

"Must be some beaver," Dad says.

We work at the debris until something catches Dad's eye. He points at a clump of sticks.

"What's that under there?" he asks.

"I can't see it," I say, and I move closer to him.

"There is something big and black under there."

He moves toward it. Struggles for balance against slick rocks and loose gravel. The water goes dark with silt we've let free.

Dad leans forward. Peers into the dirty water.

"Is it a fish?" I ask.

"No, it's not fish. It's bigger. A lot bigger."

Dad looks at me. It is only Spring, but his face is tan and his beard is tinted red from days of sun. He has furrowed his brown. His eyes are wide and brimming. It is a look I've seen only once before. In the hospital. On the last day Mom was alive.

"She'll be okay, Dad."

He'd just returned from talking with the doctor in the hallway. He leaned over Mom, kissed her lips as I'd seen him do hundreds of times, then stood and looked at me. That furrowed brow, those wide, brimming eyes.

"She's not gonna be okay," he said.

Mom had been silent for weeks. Growing smaller and colder each day. It had become part of our routine, being there at her bedside. Talking to her and talking to each other as the blue and gray hoses and the hum-beeping machines kept her body alive.

"She'll pull out of it," I said, because I always believed she would.

Dad shook his head.

I squeezed Mom's hand, kissed her cheek.

"Bye Mom. Love you. See you tomorrow."

I waited in the doorway, but Dad did not come. He kneeled at Mom's side. Touched her cheeks and her lips.

"I wish, honey," he whispered to her, "that I could see your pretty eyes again."

He moved closer to her. Kissed her. Put his face to her chest and cried. I closed the door. Walked into the wide, yellow hallway. And waited there a long time. Nurses and orderlies passed. Those that recognized me slowed and smiled. Others moved past quickly. En route to other patients in other rooms. And the longer I waited, the lonelier I felt and I began thinking of Sheila Carmichael and how much I missed her sometimes. But sitting outside my Mom's hospital room was not the place for thought like this. And besides, Sheila was now in a better place. Hundreds of miles away in Pleasanton, California. Where skin and human touch are not as sacred as they are in Michigan. And so, I thought instead of the big caramel chocolate bars I'd seen earlier that day in the cafeteria vending machine, and I wished I had a dollar to buy one for Dad and me to share.

A doctor and two nurses—none that I'd ever seen before—came to Mom's room. They smiled politely. Knocked on the door. Then went inside. I'm not sure why I didn't follow them, but something in my gut told me that there was nothing I could do but wait and stay out of the way. And so, that's what I did. For what must have been an hour. Until Dad came out of the room and closed the door behind him.

He looked better. Refreshed, if not relieved. We walked quietly down the bright hallway, out of the hospital, and into the parking lot. When we got into the truck, Dad drove us to the Lud's Restaurant drive-thru for Giantburgers, fries, and vanilla milkshakes. We ate in silence. In the truck. At Michekewis Park. We watched kids play on swings and teeter-totters. We watched whitecaps roll and break on the big lake. And before we pulled away, we opened our windows to feed leftovers to the seagulls that begged all around.

I don't remember when he told me that he'd given the order to pull the plug. But he did. It must have come out quietly. Like a secret. Hidden in our salty fingertips, the grease-soaked bags, wax paper wrappers, and the half-empty milkshake in my hand.

6.

We stand in the stream for a long time waiting for the water to clear. Dozens of suckers, lively and quick, start upstream. They dart around and between our legs.

"Help me move the rest of these sticks," Dad says. "But do it slow, so we don't cloud the water again."

We pick up sticks and toss them, one after another, onto the shore. My hands and feet ache in the icy water. I shiver as the wind rolls over Lake Huron, rattles cattails and leaves, and blows through me. The suckers keep coming. Blasting upstream like dark lightning. But something tells me that this is it. We have come here to do this and now we are done. There'll be no fishing. No spearing. No smoked suckers today.

"That's enough," Dad says. "I can see it better now."

He takes his knife from his pocket. Opens it. Plunges the shiny blade into the water.

"What is it?" I ask.

"A garbage bag," he says.

He moves his hands under the water. Pulls, cuts and tears. Pieces of plastic rise and float like little rafts downstream.

"Oh God," he says.

And as I turn to him, I see that what he's found is something that should not be.

"It's a girl," he says.

Her skin is milk white. Lips blue. Her eyes the brightest green I've ever seen and they are looking up. Past us. At the big wide sky. Seeing something we cannot see. Dad drops his knife into the water. Color rushes from his face. I close my eyes and shake my head. This does not make sense. It cannot be believed. And suddenly, there is nothing in the world but sound. Gulls eating dead fish. Waves on Lake Huron. The breeze. The trickle and rush of the stream. Blood through my veins. Dad's shallow breathing. And the sound the beaver makes as it slips into the water, cracks its mighty tail, and breaks the world in two.

a fish story

1.

Four forty-five in the morning. Stars. Satellites. Space dust. And my high beams bounce off trees, guardrails, signs. Four deer, a family of raccoons, a porcupine. My tired eyes stretch from white line to white line and I fight the urge to sleep. I've not left home in days—maybe a week—and I wouldn't be going anywhere now if it wasn't for Tom and Shelly. The only two friends I've made an effort to keep since Kali died. I think of them this morning. Up early on little sleep, or operating on no sleep at all. Loading coolers packed with ice, food, and beer into the cuddy. Stocking the liquor cabinet. Double-checking gear. Hooking their 23-foot Thompson to the tongue of their old Chevy diesel and pulling it to Knee High Harbor to meet me for our annual outing. One full day of fishing and drinking. Wide open water. Big sky. And even though I know it will be familiar and friendly, I know too, it will be hard. Not because of the questions and conversation, but because of things unspoken. Kali is gone. The world has moved on. But I am anchored and unmoving.

I think of her a long while, but it is the kind of thought that does no good—what could have been, what was, what will now always be—and these thoughts only make me want to turn around, drive home, and hide away for another long while. And so, I think of Tom and Shelly and fishing and Lake Huron, and it is this line of thought that hooks me, pulls me up through the deep and gets me believing that things might be okay. There is the water, the sun, the camaraderie—all of it new again and waiting—and this is enough, at least for today, to steer me in the right direction so that before I know it, I am five minutes from Knee High Harbor, not remembering a lick of the drive since the deer, raccoons, and porcupine.

2.

At 6:30, I reel in a salmon. Out of synch. Out of my element. I mishandle the fish and tangle it with two other lines. Shelly nets it, unhooks it, and wrestles it into the cooler. She covers it in ice, closes the lid, but the big fish thrashes, pounds, and pops the lid. Shelly laughs, shuts the cooler, sits on it, and watches as I detangle lines, re-rig them, and get them back into the water. The sky loses its last bit of dark. Stars fade. A ship moves like a shadow against the pink light of the horizon. The fish in the cooler jumps three times then stops. Shelly rises. Stretches. Then disappears into the cuddy.

Tom steers the boat. I watch the rod tips. All six of them. Arced and trembling. Shelly returns from the cuddy with a drink for each of us. She hands one to Tom. He sips it. Smiles. Kisses her cheek.

"Another perfect morning. And another perfect Seven-and-Seven," he says.

Shelly smiles and takes over the captain's seat. Tom walks over to me.

"I'm glad you came," he says.

"It's been a long time since I've been on Huron," I say.

"Probably since the accident, hey?"

Tom says this, then takes a long drink.

"Tom!" Shelly snaps. "Why would you say that?"

The sun eases up the sky. A breeze moves over us. Starts small waves. Chills the air. And there it is. The accident. The loss. My last time on Lake Huron. Pulled from the deep. Brought out into the boat for us to consider.

I pull the hood of my sweatshirt up over my head.

"It's okay," I say, and I take a drink. Tom is right. It is a perfect Seven-and-Seven.

Shelly walks over. Stands between us. Puts her arm around me.

"I wasn't sure you'd come," she says and smiles. "We sure missed you last year."

All of us are silent a moment as one of the rod tips hammers down quickly then returns to its natural curve.

"False alarm," Tom says.

Shelly waves her drink across the horizon.

"Look at it!" she beams. "This place has got *you* written all over it."

She pauses to sip her drink. I take another drink of mine.

"It's *you*," she says. "This lake, the sky, the sun. This is who you are. You need this. *We* need it."

Tom watches the rod tips. I can feel the boat turning slowly, but we are out so far and so alone that it doesn't matter. We could push along through the water, unmanned for miles, as long as we don't mind tangled lines and lost tackle.

Ice cubes rattle in Shelly's glass as she hangs her arms around me.

"Things happen, Aden. I'm sorry she's gone."

Shelly smells like wood smoke and whiskey. As usual, they've been up late the night before. Sitting at the bonfire. Drinking. Discussing what lures to use. Glow-strips at forty-five feet for early morning. Hoochie-mammas two hours into sunrise. Cowbells running deep near Gull Island if we make it to noon. And I'm sure they discussed me. Their friend gone silent. Holed up in his old country house. Reading newspapers and books. Listening to music. Watching old movies. Eating macaroni and cheese, peanut butter sandwiches, and frozen pizzas. Staring out the window at birds and dragonflies while dirty dishes and laundry pile up and grass grows high.

I want to wrap my arms around her. Bury my head in her shoulder. Hold her and just breathe, but I can't. None of us have been drinking enough for that.

Shelly holds me until she spills her drink.

"I'm sorry," she says.

She lets go. Moves to the wheel. I feel the boat straighten and I take a deep breath.

I stare at one of the rod tips. Will it to move. Wish a fish would nail the line so that there would be some distraction. Just enough so we could move on.

Tom moves close so that we stand shoulder-to-shoulder. He sips his drink. Gazes into the wake.

"When's the last time you were on a date?" he asks.

I think for a moment. Thumb back through the days since Kali. Try to remember anyone besides her, but I can't. It's not possible. And the only thing I can ever remember is the same thing I always do. That day on this lake. The morning of our one-year anniversary. Looking up through the cuddy window at a brilliant summer sky. My body filled with rest and feeling fine because I could smell her in my pillow, the sheets, and my skin.

"Come on," Tom says. "When's the last time you were on a date?"

"I haven't dated," I say.

Tom shakes his head.

I am quiet. Rocking with the motion of the boat through water and praying for the loss of balance that will send me stumbling overboard.

"Aden," Tom says, "There's someone I got in mind for you. A pretty girl from the office. Her name's Marie. A good girl. Creative type. An artist. Works in watercolors and ..."

He stops. Rubs his chin. This is something he has practiced. Thought about saying so much that he's forgotten the lines.

"Oils, Tom! Oils!" Shelly shouts over her shoulder.

Tom sips his drink.

"That's it," he says. "She works in watercolors and oils. She even has her stuff on exhibit and for sale. You can see some of it at the Knee High Museum. She's nice. A real keeper."

He reaches into his pocket. Pulls out a yellow scrap of paper. I want to be surprised. Shocked. Angered that people cannot understand that it has only been a year, but I can't. The whiskey. The water. Tom's good intentions. All of it has me numbing from the inside out.

"I invited her to come over for the barbecue tonight, but because I'm guessing you'll duck out on us, I got her number for you."

He shoves the paper into my hand, keeps talking, but I am gone. Lost in the buzz of the motor and the howl of the lines as they slice the air.

3.

Kali had been working on a children's book. We were on a weekend boat trip for our anniversary and she'd brought the draft copy for me to read. The book was about a shy little boy named Addy who was lonely because he liked to read and write instead of fish and play baseball. I'd read to the part in the story where Addy was being teased badly by the other boys. They were playing baseball, but Addy couldn't swing a bat, wasn't fast enough, and couldn't catch a fly ball. As Addy sat in the dugout contemplating a life lived unlike other boys and men, he encountered Ally. A carefree, good-spirited dragonfly with wisdom beyond her years. It was her intention to make Addy believe. In himself. His abilities. In everything.

"What do you think?" Kali asked, as she entered the cuddy.

I did not look up. I was comfortable. Content to be stretched out on my stomach with the warm sun through the skylight on my back.

"This draft is better than the last," I said. "The story is good, there is no doubt about that, but the illustrations are what make the book. The colors are amazing."

"Not the book, Aden. Me."

I rolled over, turned to look, and there she was—my wife—naked in the doorway.

"Not too bad for an old married woman," I said.

She smiled. Came forward. Leaned over me. Her soft hair brushed my face and shoulders as she kissed my lips, my cheeks, and my ears. Her breasts were soft against my skin as she kissed my neck and chest.

"Happy anniversary," she whispered.

"Oh, that's right," I said. "We're married. I thought this was a dream."

"Or maybe a nightmare."

"No, no. This is no nightmare. You haven't got fangs or bad breath."

She bit my shoulder, then nuzzled my neck.

"Fangs, yes," she said, and then kissed me. "But no bad breath."

"I like the book."

"I like you."

"You're frisky this morning."

Kali sat up and smiled at me.

"Take advantage of it," she said. "When a woman's in my condition, you never know what you're going to get."

"What condition is that?" I asked.

She sat up, patted her belly and laughed.

"The big fat baby condition," she said.

4.

The lines scream. Wind blows hard from the east. We are in three foot waves. Bouncing along under a cloudy sky. The weather has gone sour. Tom and Shelly are snuggled together on the captain's seat. Warm and rosy with drink. And I have mine. It has been one after another after another after another. I am sitting on the edge of the boat. Watching another ship. It is long, tall, and gray, and whitecaps are rolling and crashing against the hull, but the big boat is winning. Pushing along through the depths and through the waves, and I wonder what it's like for the men on board. Hours. Days. Weeks spent alone on the great inland seas. All of them there, moving from port to port for different reasons. Bills to pay. Mouths to feed. A nagging emptiness to fill. Feel. Or push away.

"How them rods doing?" Tom asks.

"Still here," I say.

"Memorize that phone number yet?" he asks.

"Not yet."

"Oh, Aden, my boy ... this Marie is the real deal. You'll love her."

He gives Shelly a big squeeze. She spills her drink.

"If I wasn't married to a honey like this, I'd call her!"

Shelly punches him in the shoulder. Kisses his cheek.

"More drinks?" she asks.

I stand. Sway on drunken sea legs. Wobble over and hand her my empty glass.

"Maybe just one more," I say.

"Another round!" Tom cheers.

Shelly goes below to mix drinks. Tom looks up at the sky.

"It'll clear up shortly. These things don't last. Once it passes, you'll see. We'll get into a mess of fish. A mess of them."

He is happy because he is in his boat with his girl and on the lake we all love. He is happy because his friend has come to fish and rise from his great depression and get on with his life. But most of all, he is happy because he is drunk. And drunk happiness is the kind that feels as if it always will last.

The sun breaks the clouds. Sunlight floods the lake. Tom steers us toward Gull Island. I brace myself against the waves.

5.

When I woke in the cuddy for the second time that morning, I stared out the small round window and thought of those things men think when they are in love and relaxed and content with their smallness in the world. Kali had gone deck side to sketch. I had fallen asleep, but only for a short while, and now I was up and reveling in the light. Feeling the gentle rock and sway of the boat as the bay came alive with small waves. I thought of Kali and me. How far we'd come in our short time. That even though we'd experienced loss and hardship in the past, this new stage of our relationship was a clear indication of things to come. That this time, our efforts and dedication—our love—would take root, grow, and last, and that this day would be the best day of our lives so far.

I listened for Kali. Her long, slender feet tapping on the deck and her humming—two things she could not help herself from doing when she sketched—but there was nothing. I sat up. Stretched. Opened the cuddy door and filled my lungs with the good lake air. I walked to the stern. Kali's sketch pad and pencils were there on the seat. Her yellow beach towel was draped over the railing near the swim ladder.

I picked up the sketch pad. She had drawn what looked to be the cover for her book.

Addy and Ally, it said. *A story of friendship and love.*

The shy little boy who did not like fishing or baseball was smiling up at the big, blue sky. And Ally, the green dragonfly, was perched on his shoulder, whispering into his ear.

I knew Kali must be feeling good. Her book was nearly done, our marriage had made it to an anniversary, and our baby was there too—invisible and unmoving, but alive and a part of us all the same. I closed the sketch pad, set it on the seat, and climbed down the swim ladder to join her.

Shelly brings more drinks. Tom has us at the drop-off near Gull Island. He's steering with his drinking hand and rubbing Shelly's shoulders with the other.

"We're marking lots of fish," Shelly says, as she taps the screen of the depth finder.

"How deep?" Tom asks.

"Sixteen," she says.

The weather has calmed, so I take off my sweatshirt and enjoy the warmth of the sun as it pushes away the clouds. Gulls and terns are blurry white dots streaking through the sky, bobbing on the water. I look to the rod tips. They are thin silver arcs of light against the green water. And there is a dragonfly. Silky-blue with big yellow eyes. Flying above the rods. Back and forth. Round and round. Until it settles on the line farthest from me. All balance and symmetry.

I take the yellow piece of paper from my pocket and stare at the numbers. Try to put them into memory. Force them deep into a new place. Beyond. Behind. Apart from the day I found my wife floating in the water. Cold and white. Only a few feet from the edge of the boat. All of the life washed out of her except the baby inside that I could not save. But I can't.

"Fish on!" Tom hollers.

He stumbles past and pulls the rod from its holder.

I look, but the dragonfly is gone. If it's ever been there at all. I throw the paper over the side. Watch it slip away into our roiling wake.

Tom shoves the rod into my hands.

"You fight this one!" he says. "Just fight and bring her in!"

opossum

1.

Another argument with my wife. And I'm speeding down M-32. Toward Gilchrist Creek in Avery. I am questioning my life. My marriage. The man I've become. And out of nowhere comes the opossum.

I see it clearly. As if watching with a zoom lens from a cloud. It ambles out of the tall grass in the ditch. Crosses the wide gravel shoulder and moves onto the black asphalt. It looks like a big dirty-white dishrag with legs.

And so.

There is the car. Fueled with emotion and traveling too fast. And there is the opossum. Suddenly still and waiting in the road. I don't stop or even slow down. The opossum is only a bump in the road. I have someplace to go. I have to get away. And this rat—this stupid marsupial—cannot be enough to set me off course and will not get in my way. But, as all unexpected things do, it does, and it isn't long before guilt has seized me, filled me with regret, and I am imagining the poor opossum. Mangled. Broken. Shards of bone. Purple guts. Pink muscle bursting through skin. Blood pooling on the road. And black eyes staring into the big morning sky. The opossum is paralyzed. Coursing with fear. Praying for a quick end to come with the next passerby.

Killing an oversized rodent—a goony-eyed trash eater—shouldn't mean anything. I've killed before. As a kid. Knocking off birds and squirrels with slingshots and BBs. As an adult. Shooting deer and rabbits with rifles and shotguns. And all of my life catching fish. With rod and reel. Nets. Spears. And by hand. But there is something about hitting this opossum that bothers me. I haven't been careful. I haven't been paying attention. I've been driving a familiar road but I'm lost as can be. And what's worst that I've done it and kept right on going.

I convince myself that what I've done is necessary. Somehow, in the greater scheme of things, I've played a part in something bigger. Lasting and complex. It is part of Mother Nature's plan. God's fancy. It is important. Another piece in the puzzle. A vital step in the evolution of the animal kingdom. A strengthening of the opossum race. Opossums aren't supposed to be crossing roads during daylight hours. They're supposed to be sleeping. So this one must have been sick. Injured. Or stupid. And now, the world has one less of them. I have done my duty. Survival of the fittest carries on.

Besides, there are other things on my mind.

Like my wife.

Temporarily insane from pregnancy. She's kicked me out of the house. Again. This time because I suggested we go walking.

"I don't want to go walking!" she snapped.

"Listen, Hannah. I'm worried. Worried about you. And worried about the baby. Sitting around like this isn't good. Why don't we exercise in the morning like we used to?"

"*I* used to exercise. *You* stumbled along behind. And that's only when I was able to get you out of bed."

She chomped at a doughnut. Glared at me.

This was true. Hannah had always tried to drag me out of bed. She was cheerful. Invigorated. Ready to go. Shaking me awake. Snatching my pillow. Trying to get me as excited about the three-mile trek to Duck Park as she was. So, every other morning, I'd go along. Stay with her as best I could. For a mile. Maybe two. But it wouldn't last long. I'd peter out. Fall behind. And end up waving her on as I turned back home.

Of course, as soon as I'd tuck myself back into bed, put my head to the pillow and find dreamland, Hannah would return. Sweaty. Breathing heavy. More energized than ever. Ready for a bout of sex. Determined to give me a workout one way or the other. Yes, my dear Hannah, she was fit. Good spirited. Fun.

Nothing like the depressed, tired woman she'd become. Spending day-after-day on the sofa. Stewing our kid in chocolate milk, junk food, and bad TV.

"Hannah. Our kid's not even seen the light of day and already you're turning it into a couch potato."

She was silent.

"Hannah?"

She bit off a chunk of doughnut. Chewed slowly. Turned off the television and stared at me. Tears started in her eyes.

"Hannah?"

"Why don't you try having this fucking kid?" she screamed. And then she threw the doughnut at me.

My attempts to calm her were useless. The more I talked, the madder she got. A pillow. The chocolate milk carton. The remote for the TV. Each flying at me with startling accuracy and speed. I ducked and dodged. Ran until I was safe outside. And I tried to imagine what the kid must have been feeling. Body temperature rising. Heartbeat racing. Surrounded by and sloshing around in fluid. Blinded and ready to become whatever Hannah and I wanted it to be. A strong little girl. A playful little boy. Growing within and alongside the lines we'd drawn and the footprints we'd left behind. To become a good person. A beautiful woman. A thoughtful man.

I stood outside. Breathed. Found comfort in the late afternoon sky as the biggest flock of blackbirds I'd ever seen—a wide swirling wave—swooped over the house and settled with an airy whoosh into the leafy crown of the big Maple in our yard. It was something special, I thought. The sort of thing I'd want to share with my kid one day. Around a campfire. At the dinner table. Riding in the car on our way to Gilchrist Creek.

"I remember the biggest flock of birds," I'd say. "They came swooping round and settled into the big Maple just as I'd ducked outside to escape being hit by the remote for the TV. You see, your Mom had kicked me out of the house again and …"

I was gone away in it—reveling in memories to come—when Hannah opened the door.

"Get out!" she screamed. She threw my fishing rod and the car keys.

The blackbirds blazed into the sky. All sound and fury. I turned toward Hannah. Pointed at the dark wave of birds rolling through the sky, but she didn't care. She threw my tackle box and creel into the yard.

"Asshole!" she screamed.

And she slammed the door.

2.

I walk upstream. Slowly. Casting wax worms weighted with small split shots. There are sparrows and jays. Otters and muskrats. And there are trout. Brookies buried in dark water that rushes over a log jam then grows deep as it carves away at a sandy bank and makes a ninety degree curve around a giant fallen cedar.

I catch two fat-bellied Brookies within five minutes. I hook the third as a canoe floats round the bend toward me. It's an old couple. Wearing floppy-brimmed sun hats. Polarized glasses. Matching blue vests. They near the log jam and steer toward the bank. I land the fish, unhook it, and place it into my creel. The woman is in the front of the canoe and gets out first. When she's ashore, she reaches over and steadies the canoe so he can get out. Their movements are fluid—synchronized—and as they lift the canoe from the water and carry it alongside the stream, I can tell they've been doing this for years. They have not noticed me, or chosen not to, as I bait my hook and cast another hapless wax worm into the deep. Behind me, I hear them put the canoe back into the water. When I turn to look, they are gliding away effortlessly. Another trout bites. I set the hook. The fish leaps from the water, shakes loose, and is gone.

I have only waded thirty yards into the stream. Have not gone any further than the log jam. But the day has passed. And I've caught five legal fish that need ice. So, I pack up and head to the car.

3.

By the time I reach the gas station in Avery, it is dark. I call Hannah to see how it will be when I get home.

"How was it?" she asks.

"It was nice," I say, looking into the sky.

The stars are so tiny and bright against all of the black that I feel far away from everything.

"Did you catch anything?"

"Brookies."

"Did you keep any?"

"More than I should have. They're in the cooler. In the trunk."

"Where are you calling from?"

"Gas station in Avery."

"Good. Then you aren't far away."

"How are you feeling?" I ask. But I know it doesn't matter. She can be fine now. Nice. Full of love and care and respect. But it can and will change without notice. I can say stupid things, nice things, mean things, lovely things, but ultimately it boils down to how she hears whatever I say. Women are mysterious, complex creatures, and I have swallowed the hard fact that I will never know the right things to ask or say. There is nothing I can do but try. Stay alert. And listen.

Hannah pauses. Takes a long deep breath.

I imagine oxygen mixing with blood. Being carried through her body. Down to our baby.

"I'm feeling fine," she says. "Sorry for kicking you out."

Another pause. Another deep breath.

I wonder how it feels. Down there. Tucked away in a world away from the world. Floating naked in a warm sea of vibration and muffled sound.

I look around the station lot. Two figures move in the shadows behind the store. I see the glow of a cigarette as they pass it back and forth.

"It's okay, Hannah. I needed some time to myself. Besides, now we've got trout to eat."

"I'll cook them when you get home," she says. "You're probably hungry."

I am hungry. And it is one of the reasons I've stopped at the station. They have venison jerky, pickled eggs, and beer. But food and drink isn't the only reason I've stopped. I also need ice for the trout in the cooler. And then there is the car. Hannah's car as much as mine, and taking it home dented, scratched, or stamped with opossum blood will easily send her into a frenzy. I want to give the car the once-over and run it through the car wash if I have to. I did not look when I stopped to fish at Gilchrist Creek because I did not want the opossum following me. Not into the stream. Not watching from the banks. And not hiding inside my creel. And now, in the glow of the station lights, I'm sure I'll find something. Blood. Guts. Hair. Bits of Mr. Opossum somewhere.

"It's getting late," I say. "I'll get something here and eat it on the way home."

"Are you sure?"

"I'm sure."

"Hurry home," she says. "I miss you."

Sure, I think. Until I get home, say something stupid, and get pelted with a shoe. A glass. The TV Guide.

"I'll hurry," I say, and I hang up the phone.

The two figures from the darkness come into the light. They are teenagers. A tall lanky one and a short stocky one. The tall one struts inside. The short one ambles toward the gas pump. Empty milk jug in hand.

I get down on my knees to survey the car for damage. There is not a mark. A drop. A shred of evidence to be found. And now, I wonder if any of it happened at all. People under great stress sometimes imagine things. So maybe I created the opossum. Maybe Mr. Opossum never existed at all. And maybe I'm just a man out for a ride in the dark with nothing but headlights and stars to guide me. And then, before I drift too far away into a place that is often hard to come back from, I see it. A bright shiny quarter near the front passenger side tire of the car.

I pick it up. It is dated 1973. The year I was born. I put it into my pocket then walk to the store. When I pass the stocky kid at the pump he is filling the milk jug with gasoline. He mumbles under his breath.

"Fuckin' opossum."

But this cannot be. There is fear—something I've not felt in a long time—rising inside of me. An uneasiness that ices my guts, turns hot, then rushes up my throat to burn.

"Beer," I say, as I walk inside. "I need beer."

The tall lanky kid is leaning against the counter waiting for the cashier. The cashier, as far as I can tell, is in a small room behind the counter. I can hear someone in there, anyway. Fumbling around. Moving boxes as if searching for something. I'm walking to the cooler at the back of the store, when I hear her shout.

"No, I'm sorry! We don't have any matches!"

"Last time I was here they gave me free ones!" the kid shouts back.

I take a bag of ice from one cooler and a six-pack of beer from another. When I get to the counter, the kid is still there. He is taller and lankier than he first appeared. Smells like pot and motor oil. His hands and wrists are grimy. It looks as if he's been under the hood of an old car all day.

The cashier is still in that back room. Only now, I can see her. Opening drawers and closing drawers. Moving boxes around. There is a small table with a microwave. A refrigerator. Coffee maker. And a big black safe. The lanky kid is leaning forward over the counter. Twitching. One hand deep into his pocket. The other tapping dirty fingernails on the counter.

When the cashier backs out of the room, she pulls the door closed and locks it with the key that's hanging from a lanyard around her neck. She turns and moves to her place behind the register. She is pregnant. Her round, firm belly juts out from under her blue AVERY DEPOT smock like an enormous balloon.

"No, I'm sorry. No matches back there."

"Then ring up the gas," the lanky kid says, nodding toward the window. The stocky kid has finished filling the jug. He's standing at the pump, staring at us.

"You're not supposed to put gas into milk jugs," she says, as she punches the register keys. "It's not an approved container."

She is tiny and young and doesn't even look old enough to be working the night shift. She has a nice, pleasant face, green eyes, and wild frizzy red hair.

"We ran out of gas just down the road," Lanky says. "It's the only thing we could find."

"Two dollars and ninety-eight cents," the cashier says.

She looks out at the stocky kid. He's lit a cigarette and is leaning against a NO SMOKING sign as he blows smoke rings.

"Can't he read?" she asks.

Lanky takes his hand from deep in his pocket and dumps a

handful of change onto the counter.

"Fuck off," he says.

The cashier scrambles after coins as they bounce and roll. The lanky kid struts away. Heads outside to join his stocky companion.

She counts the change as she drops it into the cash drawer.

"Two seventy-three," she says. "That brat shorted me twenty-five cents!"

I set the beer and the ice on the counter. Watch Lanky and Stocky disappear into the darkness. Take the shiny 1973 from my pocket and give it to her.

She smiles a crooked smile. Does not show her teeth. And I wonder what she's hiding because Hannah's smile is the same. Crooked and never wide because she's got two upper front falsies in place of the two teeth that got knocked out when she was just a kid. A dare, a mishap, too much fun on the playground swings. And now, she lives a life of crooked smiles. Trying to hide two teeth that are never as white and natural looking as the real thing.

The cashier drops the quarter into register then rings up the beer and the ice.

"Anything else?" she asks.

"Two of those jerky sticks," I say, nodding toward a big jar behind the counter.

She gets out the tongs, a wax paper bag, and puts three of the biggest sticks into it.

"Enough?" she asks.

"And a pickled egg," I say.

She giggles. Flashes that crooked smile.

"You pregnant too?"

"No. But my wife is."

She puts two eggs into another wax bag. Tallies up the total. Finally, I notice her nametag. KATIE, it says.

"How far along is she?" Katie asks.

"Due any minute."

I place the money into her hand. Notice that she's not wearing a wedding band.

"How far along are you?" I ask.

"Too far."

We exchange smiles. I gather up my goods and walk out.

When I get to the car I open the trunk and then open the cooler. One of the trout looks like it's still breathing, but I know this cannot be. I have knocked each of them in the head with the handle of a knife and I have gutted them. All the fish are dead. I am only seeing what I want to see. Gills in. Gills out. Tails back and forth. The fish still alive. Free in the stream.

I dump ice onto the fish until I see them no more and I put four of the beers into the cooler because I will drink two on the ride home. I shut the cooler and close the trunk. I stand in the parking lot under the station lights eating the pickled egg, holding the beer. I want to open a bottle and guzzle it down, but I can feel Katie looking at me through the window and it feels like Hannah is there too. Watching my every move.

4.

Hannah and I had been drinking a lot at the outset of the pregnancy. It had worried her deeply.

"It'll have Down's Syndrome," she said. "And what if the doctor says so? I can't get an abortion, can I?"

She was curled up next to me on the couch, sobbing all over. I wasn't sure of what to say, so I said nothing.

"You'll resent me and you'll hate me because we won't have a perfect baby," Hannah cried.

"It was only a few beers," I said, as I took a drink from the bottle I was holding. "A little beer never hurt anyone. Especially not a kid. They're resilient."

"You don't understand," she said.

"What's to understand? Everything will be fine."

"You always say that."

And everything is always fine, isn't it?"

She was silent, but I could feel that something was building inside of her.

"Hannah?"

She stood. Clenched her fists.

"You don't even know me!"

"But I do know you and I know that you're hurt and that you are worried and ..."

And before I could finish my sentence, one of her fists came at me. I blocked the punch with my hand.

"Get out!" she screamed. "Get out of here right now!"

Veins rose in her temples and her neck. Her wide eyes glared at me. I moved forward to try and hold her, but she took another swing. This time she connected, landing her fist squarely on my cheek. I stepped away, and for a moment we were silent. Eyeing each other. Up and down. Two wild animals. Caged.

That had been our first argument. The first time she'd kicked me out. The first time I'd disappeared to Avery for some time alone. When I believed it would change. That we would change. That people were shaped and smoothed over time. Like stones in and out of the water on the shoreline. But, as it turns out, life is not like that. Not for us. Not yet. We are still rough around the edges. Taking the waves as they come.

5.

I eat the pickled egg. Get into the car. Glance over at the store window and Katie is there watching. I wave to her. Start the engine. She doesn't wave back. I put one of the bottles into the cup holder and open the other. Take several long drinks. Cram it between my legs for safekeeping. Then move onto the road.

Yellow lines blur and dash alongside the car. The sky is more blue than black. Stars flash and twinkle. I don't want to go home. I want to turn around. Head back toward Katie and Avery. To the stream and the trout. And I want to keep going. Beyond all I have known so that I can know more. More than Hannah. More than our married life. More than being alone. And suddenly, ahead of me, there is a small light in the road.

I slow the car. See the orange flames. And recognize the two shadows. Tall and lanky. Short and stocky. Standing at the fire. When they realize that the headlights are growing closer—slowing to a stop—they stomp out the fire. Throw down the milk jug. And run off through the ditch into the dark woods.

I stop alongside the smoldering heap, but I don't get out of the car. Even with the windows up and pickled egg and beer on my breath, the stench of the fire works its way into the car. And then, the sight of the opossum there—her body curled up, burned black, legs clinging to babies against her belly—strikes me so deep that I know it is something I will never share.

Not with my wife, as I shake from the inside out and prepare the trout for the freezer.

And never with my child. My spring of hope that pushes the pedal to the floor and sends me down the road. Back home. Where I belong.

blackbirds

Little Man climbs a rock near the flower garden. Stands on it and waves.

"Hi, Mommy! Hi, Daddy!"

He waves. We wave.

"Watch me!" he says.

He swings his arms as he yells, "One … two … three!" then dives into the grass, an ocean, a bowl of pudding—whatever it is his three-year old mind sees—and he lands on his hands and knees, laughing. It is so fun and exciting that he climbs to do it again and again.

We are on the porch. Reveling in the warmth of the day. Relaxing in our chairs.

"Good wine," I say.

S.B. smiles.

"Sure is."

I take a drink, savor it, and look around the neighborhood. The world is green. Flowers blooming. People are out and about. Riding bikes. Doing yard work. Sitting on porches and decks, lawn chairs and steps. Birds chatter. Wind chimes sing. Kids scream, squeal and shout, as they play in backyards, on front lawns, on sidewalks, and in streets. Dogs bark. Lawn mowers buzz. Weed-whackers whir. And one block north of us, the old conversion van turned ice cream truck sounds *Pop Goes the Weasel.*

"Another beautiful day," I say.

S.B. smiles. Brushes a long dangling curl from her bright green eyes. Radiates sunshine.

"I'm glad we have this porch," she says.

I look at the worn, uneven floorboards, nail heads rising from the wood like daisies to the sun, and a mile-long list unravels in my head. There is the porch to repair and paint, but there is so much more. Kitchen cupboards to update. Crawlspace to insulate. Cracked living room window. Drafty door jambs. Old pipes breaking down, leaking secrets, rotting two-by-fours and cracking walls. All the projects—big and small—fester under my skin. But I don't want to think of them or talk about them. It is too nice. A lazy warm day. And I'm relaxing with my wife. This is not the time to feel the weight of anything, except the wine glass in my hand.

I have a look, S.B. says, when I'm thinking too much. And it is this look that I must be showing because she quickly snaps me back to reality.

"Let's not think about work," she says. "Let's just be here on the porch, enjoy the warmth, and drink our cheap wine."

As she says this, the giant shadow of a bird sweeps over our yard. Little Man watches the black shape roll over the sidewalk, glide over the grass, and move steadily toward him. He is not sure what to do and looks helpless as he stands atop the garden rock. He is an ant on a pebble and a big foot is coming down. He is a squirrel on a surfboard, adrift in shark-infested waters. He is a little boy. Unfamiliar with the workings of light and dark, and he is a little worried as the shadow nears.

He clenches his eyes shut. Waits. And the shadow passes over. It is hard to know what he expects. Feels. What he sees. He could be thirty feet in the air by now. High above, in the grasp of soft claws or furry paws, looking down on Mom and Dad. He could be inside the belly of a goldfish, swimming with turtles, riding through clouds on top of a whale. Wherever he's gone to, he is smiling and still, and is at peace with the world. I want to capture the moment. The way it makes me feel. And I want to bottle it. Keep it. And on days when he's grown and on to bigger and better things, I want to sit on the porch with S.B. and have a glass of how things used to be. But for now, there is only my boy, opening his eyes, searching the rock, the grass, his shirt sleeves and pants pockets for the big shadow that's come and gone.

"That's a lot of black feathers," says S.B.

The big long-tailed blackbird has flown across the street and landed on the peak of the neighbor's house.

"That's a wide-open field-and-stream kind of bird," I say.

"He must be passing through," says S.B.

Indeed, we are used to robins and chickadees. Blue-jays and sparrows. Not a bird like this. Just outside the city there are fields, state parks, miles of shoreline. So it is likely we are only a stop along the way. But all travelers stop for similar reasons, and immediately it is clear what this dark giant has come for. The blackbird is watching two robins. The robins are taking turns tending their nest in a big cottonwood. While one waits, the other flies to the ground.

"Feeding time," I say.

The robin in the grass nabs a cricket and flies to the nest. The other robin starts down. This routine continues for several minutes. One up at the nest. One after bugs on the ground. S.B. and I drink up our glasses, refill, and watch Little Man learn the art of playing on his own.

He peels a black chunk of something from the bottom of his shoe. Moves it toward his mouth.

"Don't eat that!" we shout in unison.

He laughs, throws whatever-it-is into the lawn.

"What if we hadn't been looking?" asks S.B.

I think on that a moment. Imagine him shoving all sorts of things in his pie hole. Gravel, dog shit, rusty nails.

"He probably eats all sorts of things," I say.

S.B. scrunches her face. Shakes her head. Takes another drink.

The blackbird hops along the neighbor's roof. Moves closer to the cottonwood. The robins continue up and down.

"I've got a bad feeling," says S.B.

"About what?"

"The babies," she says, and she motions toward the cottonwood.

The robin in the grass has wrestled a big worm from the ground and has started toward the nest. As it lands in the tree, the worm wriggles free and falls to the ground. Both robins fly after it.

S.B. gasps.

"The nest," she says.

I imagine what it must be like. Up in that nest. Watching, as a big dark figure sails from the rooftop. Blocks the warm sun. Swoops down. It is an airplane, a kite, a dinosaur. And it pauses only a second before plucking me from my nest, forcing me into the cold of the bright airy sky.

"Is that blackbird doing what I think it is?"

"Yes," I say.

"Is that what they do?"

"Sometimes."

The blackbird flies the baby robin across the yard. Lands in tall grass below a feeder near the neighbor's house. It holds the baby with one talon, balances with the other, and slowly tears the baby apart. The robins chirp and charge, rise and dive. But the blackbird does not move. Then suddenly, there comes another. Just as big. Perched on a stump near the cottonwood. Watching the scene unfold.

Little Man looks at us, then across the street.

"Birds?" he says.

I look to S.B. Her smile is gone. She's holding her wine tightly. Tapping her wedding band against the glass.

"If it was our yard, we could do something," she says.

I get up.

"I can go over there if you want."

"No, honey. Sit down. It's probably too late."

I look at the blackbird on the stump. Then up at the cottonwood. There are more babies up there. Moving around in the nest and I can't help but think they are doomed.

Little Man is back at the rock. Climbing up. Jumping down. Clapping his hands.

"Yea, Mommy! Yea, Daddy!"

S.B. glances at him, smiles, but quickly returns to the birds.

The ice cream truck rounds the corner, shuts off the music, and stops at the end of the block. A throng of half-naked children files out of a little yellow car. They are dressed in bathing suits. Two of them are wearing water wings. One is sporting a snorkel and a mask.

"Look at that," I say.

Finally, she breaks from the birds.

"There's not a beach for miles."

"Must be a pool party," I say.

The kids line up. All of them get cones then run back to the car. Except for one. A little red-headed girl. Probably five years old. Wearing a bikini. Bracelets. So much makeup, I can see it from our place six houses down. She reaches up to the window. A big, hairy arm reaches down. Hands her a red Popsicle, then strokes her cheek.

"That's a little weird," S.B. says.

The other arm comes out. Reaches to touch her hair and the little girl slaps it away. She stomps her feet. Shakes her finger at the van, then runs to the car. She gets in. The car moves ahead, but only a few feet before it stops.

Shadows move inside the car. There is a great commotion. A man steps out.

He is pale. Skinny. Wearing black shorts, white socks, and sandals. He has no shirt, but the way the sun has tanned his arms, face and neck, it looks like he's wearing one. A bright, blinding white shirt with two little dark buttons where his nipples are. He walks to the ice cream truck. The big arms come out and rest on the window ledge. The man from the car says something—places an order, I guess—then stands there waiting as the arms disappear into the truck.

S.B. drinks her wine. Stands and leans on the railing.

"There's something funny going on," she says.

The man from the car looks up and down the street. Shifts side-to-side on his sandals. One of the big hairy arms returns to the window and offers a tall drink. The man takes it, rears back as if winding up for a pitch, then throws it into the ice cream truck. He does not wait for a response. Does not say a word. He simply turns, walks to his car, and opens the door. The children cheer.

S.B. looks at me. We smile.

"Quite the scene!" Harry says, as he walks up to our porch. He is our neighbor. A good, solid man who walks and bikes and gardens. He is thin and fit and has the best looking yard on the block. Lush green grass. Flowers always in bloom. And he keeps us stocked—all summer long—with the best tomatoes in the world.

"Which scene is that?" I ask.

"The guy at the ice cream truck."

"Oh yes, hell of a scene."

The yellow car glides past. The driver is grinning. The kids are laughing. The little red-headed girl is wearing mirrored sunglasses, licking her Popsicle, but is not too busy to wave. S.B., Harry, and I all wave. Even Little Man, from his place atop the rock, waves.

"Kids!" he shouts.

Harry lines up tomatoes on the railing next to S.B.

"That guy in the van is bad news," he says.

"He never comes down this way," says S.B.

"No, ma'am, and he won't. That's as far as he'll go."

Harry glares at the ice cream truck. Veins rise and pulse in his neck.

"Uh-oh," I say. "Did something happen?"

S.B. elbows my ribs.

"That ice cream truck stopped in front of our house last summer," Harry says. "The driver reached out and touched my boy just like he touched that girl."

"Oh my," says S.B.

I elbow her.

"It wasn't right. I knew it wasn't right, but before I could do anything, the van was pulling away."

"Probably a good thing you didn't get hold of him," I say.

"But I did," Harry says, "I got him."

He clenches his right hand into a fist. Steadies it at his side. S.B. and I glance at each other. Sip our wine.

"When my boy came inside and told me that pervert asked if he wanted to go for a ride, I went straight for my baseball bat."

"Oh dear," says S.B.

"I ran out the door and around the block until I caught that cocksucker and then I smashed out all of his fucking lights!"

Harry is suddenly red-faced. Perspiration peppers his forehead. His eyes have gone black. S.B. and I look to Little Man. He is busy climbing rocks and hasn't heard a word.

The ice cream truck starts, moves ahead, turns the corner. I notice for the first time, gray duct tape on the taillights.

"No folks, we don't have to worry about that ice cream truck coming around here."

Harry relaxes his fist. Shakes his head clear. Smiles at us. We smile and nod, and then we are silent. There is only the sound of the wind chimes, Little Man playing, and the frantic robins.

One blackbird is still at it, tearing apart the baby bird. The other is up in the cottonwood, making its way toward the nest.

"That's a shame," Harry says, nodding toward the birds.

"Awful," says S.B.

"Nature's a bitch," Harry says.

He picks one of the tomatoes off the railing. Turns it around and around with his long fingers. It is a beautiful tomato. I'm looking forward to slicing it. Salting it. Savoring each bite.

"I grow 'em right out the top of my compost pile," he says.

S.B. and I exchange smiles. Take drinks.

The robins have finally scared off the blackbird. One of them stands over the dead baby and flaps its wings. The other hops and bobs and pecks the ground. Harry looks up at the cottonwood. The other blackbird inches toward the nest.

Harry steps away from the porch. Holds the tomato. Rears back and launches it across the street, up into the cottonwood. It misses the blackbird by only a foot. Hits the thick gray trunk and explodes like a red bomb. The blackbird flies up and away into the clear blue sky. The robins returns to the nest.

"Yea!" Little Man cheers.

"Yea!" we cheer.

And a couple streets over, the old conversion van turned ice cream truck sounds *Pop Goes the Weasel* as it continues its rounds.

THE REALITY

an introduction

It is January 2012. Little Man had another hellacious day at school. Oogie will not go to sleep. S.B. is beat. I'm ready for a long, restful sleep. But from the sounds of things a little after 8, Tuesday night on 2nd Avenue—with wailing kids and barking dogs—I can see there'll be no rest. Not tonight. Not anytime soon. And any rest we do get will only be a slight break in the action. A pause of motion. A blip in time. And though it will be welcomed when it comes, it really doesn't mean anything because when we wake one day to find that the hands of time have pushed us along and along, we don't remember the sleep. We remember these—the moments, the scenes, the feelings of the day—and because I want to remember as much as I can for as long as possible, I have written them down.

For Little Man.

For Oogie.

For S.B.

So that all of us can be together and last and be thankful for the great gift of family that we've been given to share.

~ K.J.

cutting teeth

One robin piping over the noise of jets and cars and I wish there were thousands more to drown this goddamned city. And cougars to attack crooks. Wolves to devour rapists. Woolly mammoths to stampede child molesters. And grizzlies to attack these ignorant fucks that believe they are tough and entitled and that the rules— for them—do not apply. But there aren't enough robins. And there aren't any cougars, wolves, woolly mammoths, or grizzlies to be found. And so, I come here. A big glass of wine. Head brimming. And fingers heavy to the keys. It's best I don't think of the city, these stupid people, my desire to leave, and I just get right to the words.

Jovi cut her first tooth today. It is her secret. She does not willingly show it. But it is there. A small white line through the gum. I never imagined it would be so important. So significant. That one day, I'd be at work, sitting in my blue-gray cubicle editing words of people smarter than I'll ever be, and my wife would send me a text message.

"Jovi got a tooth!"

And I would feel only pure joy. Heavy warmth deep in my gut rising up and that it would be so strong it would nearly choke me. But that's how it was. How it came. How it is and always will be.

My daughter's little tooth carried me through the day.

I know it is only a tooth. That millions of kids get them and lose them and that all of us have them. I know it is nothing. But by God, it is *something*. And I'm happy. Happy because she is my little girl with big blue eyes and a sunny disposition and happy because every time I look at her, I am thankful for love and direction and trial and error and the great big hands that are working behind the scenes to help us find the right path. And I'm happy because Monday was grand with light and warmth and I got up early and exercised and wrote a little and my wife was up early and saw me off to work. And when the work day was done, I drove home and all of us had supper together. When we finished, we took a two-mile walk, then returned home to play basketball in the driveway.

Finally, as the sun started to drop and crickets came to life and the city began to wind down, we sat on the steps of the porch and fed bread to the mallards that keep coming round at 7:08 every evening. And the day stayed strong and true even as I smelled the death nearby.

I looked to S.B.

"I smell it," she said.

I thought maybe it was something under the porch. Or rotting sparrow eggs in the gutters. Or that one of the trash stealing raccoons had been hit and was dead in the tall grass on the other side of the road. But the kids were watching the ducks, I was tossing bread, and the moment was sweet enough to let on as if there was nothing.

"Over there," S.B. said to me, as she handed bread to Little Man and bounced Jovi on her knee. She nodded to a tuft of grass, near the cedar bush, only three feet away.

"Must have flown into the window," I said.

It was a blackbird. A broken neck. Feathers still shimmering. Black-blue-and green in the dying daylight.

Little Man threw bread at the ducks. Jovi pierced the sky with her big blue eyes.

I plucked a leaf from the Hosta plant and used it like a tissue to pick the dead bird from the grass. An ant crawled out of its eye socket. Another out of its beak. I brushed them away, wrapped the body in the leaf, and made the trip to the mulch pile like I've done all the other times.

A baby blue jay that S.B. found last year just outside the front door.

A dead mouse in the garage.

A dead sparrow by the cottonwood.

A dead robin in the flower bed.

A garter snake flattened on the road.

And a chipmunk that was not yet dead, but that I had to put out of its misery because the cat had cut it badly and tore off a leg.

Our mulch pile is rich with dark soil that has grown worms so big that if you used them for fishing, you wouldn't need a hook. Such a worm would surely grab the fish and wrestle it in. I imagine if we planted a garden in that soil our vegetables would be in the *Guinness Book of World Records*.

But I don't want to be famous for having the biggest cucumber. Or pumpkin. Or beanstalk. I just want to write stories. Love my wife. My kids. And believe that there is more to all of this than the city and its people who've become so disconnected from the truth.

Tonight, with these thoughts, these feelings, these fingers to the keys, I wish we could just get out of here. Have space. Breathe. But for now, we are here. In a place that does not sleep. With its whirring traffic, rumbling jets. And I must be patient and hopeful, so we keep doing what it takes. To keep the faith. Make ends meet. And revel in this beauty of cutting teeth.

gauge life by your gut

You'll have your wife and kids. Your job. You'll have your responsibilities. Past-times. Things you like to do. But in the end— or at the end—all you will ever have is yourself. You wear the Hubby, Daddy, and Provider hats. And you are all of those things, but you are none of them as well. And you'll realize this on the eve of your 37th birthday after a day of work, spicy chicken wings, double chocolate cake, three beers, and four glasses of wine. And because your wife is tired and has celebrated enough for the day, you'll end up pouring one more glass of wine and going out into the rainy night, out of the house and into the studio. The little room you built for her because you love her and because she loves to paint and because you want only for her to be happy. And you will feel a little sad because alcohol is a depressant—you learned this many years ago in Sociology class and from seeing people you love go nuts on three-day benders—but it will not stop you from hitting the keys. Digging deep. Trying to make sense out of your birthday. Just another day. Meaningless. Stupid, really. Maybe not to your Mom. The woman that gave up her life to have you at seventeen. The woman that had to go back to school to get her diploma because you popped out on the day she was supposed to graduate. And maybe not to your Dad. The man that turned his life around, gave up drinking and benders and fighting to raise you to know right from wrong and gauge life by your gut. And definitely not to your wife and kids. The three people that look forward to seeing you every day you pull into the driveway after work. But to you, in the hollow place that really matters, you know you are just another speck. A nothing. And sometimes it feels good to think of what it would be like to say fuck it, move away from everyone, live in a cabin in the woods, and write stories that nobody will ever read.

But it's best not to long for things you do not have when you are married, have kids, and are living a good, quiet life in the city. And the only reason you are feeling like this—being so self-involved on your birthday—is because you've been drinking and because deep down—just below that river of responsibility—you want to be more than you are. For them. For yourself. For everybody. But you've eaten too much. Drank enough for two days. And you are writing with balls bigger than you'll ever have. So, to keep things in check, stay comfortable in your routine, and in step with expectations, you will do this:

Wrap up the writing. Put away the wine. And you'll go inside. Pass by the snacks sleeping in cupboards and the cold cuts resting in the fridge. Walk past the living room and the promises of late night TV. And into the bathroom you'll go. To flush the system. Wash your face. Brush your teeth. And then, it's off to the bedroom. Like a good little boy. Under the covers. Next to your warm wife. And you will sleep. Soundly. Until morning. When the birds, then your kids and wife wake. And it is a new day. One that you must remember belongs to everyone.

the good that comes from small things

Probably need to finish this glass of wine. Have another. Then get back here. To the keys. Thoughts. Sounds of the city winding down. And come up with something. But some nights there is nothing. And it's all I can do to drift the surface, dragging bait along the bottom. Unaware of the world. Locked on to the sound of water. The big blue sky. And the nothing that I wish could consume me. Because I'm tired. Tired of working to make ends meet. Tired of fighting the good fight. Tired of banging away and banging away and banging away and getting nothing but more tired and more empty.

But it is not good to write about being tired and empty when I have people counting on me. My patient wife. My jovial daughter. My son, the Little Man. And it is not good to wish we were somewhere else. In a place we cannot be because we are not in the appropriate tax bracket. And even though I know that money and belongings and things don't matter, I wish to hell we had more money, had quality belongings, and we were living a life where money didn't matter.

We have love. There is no doubt about that. We are strong. Faithful. Caring. We are staying upright. Keeping chins up. Keeping at the keepin' on. But sometimes all of that just isn't enough.

I want a house in a small town. To be near the water. In the trees. I want to raise our kids where they can run free. Spend time with their grandparents. Believe in the good that comes from small things. Like chopping wood. Planting gardens. Catching fish. Picking mushrooms and strawberries. Building tree forts. And learning about leaves and birds and the stars. About God and Hope and Truth and doing what you love no matter what anyone says.

Like this. Coming here. To you. My old friend. The one that has never judged, forgotten, or given up on me. Because like me, you believe that heart comes from hard knocks, hard work, and giving more than you receive.

safe and sound

Another day rounding home plate and I wonder where it goes. Seconds to minutes. Minutes to hours. Sun up to sun down. And as the big orange ball falls slow and heavy beyond the treetops, I am thankful that I got to be part of another one. It was another good day in this good life. And no matter how many things may have gone astray—not many did—it was another day to remember.

And because memories don't last, I'm putting this one down. Fingers to keys. Characters to paper. So that one day I'll have it to read.

It's important to look back. Take stock. Gain perspective. Important to latch on to the past so that we can savor today. And lately, I haven't been savoring much. Too many things running through my brain. Too much I want to get done. And never ever enough time. But I'll get the hang of it. I'll learn not to think so much. Or, at the very least, I'll finally understand that I can only do so much and that some days there's no sense doing anything because doing only makes me tired and forgetful and longing for more than I have. And being tired and forgetting and wanting more than I have does nothing but make the wheels spin and spin and spin. All motion and no movement. All thought, but no ideas. Lots of journal writing, but no stories. And stories are what should be paying the bills.

But let's not think about bills and let's not think of using something so beautiful for shit. The important part of doing this— coming here and banging away—is to keep moving forward. To keep at the keepin' on. To keep believing. And most of all, it is for me to stop. Take a look around. Listen. And realize that the best life I'll ever have is the one I'm smack dab in the middle of. Wife and kids. Dogs and cats. Little house in the garden city. All fueled up on possibility, but firmly rooted in family. Wiping tears, noses, and butts. Holding hands. Hugs and kisses. Playing catch. Peek-a-boo. Doing whatever it takes to make my family happy. Safe and sound.

responsibility and expectation

Heat off concrete. Sun going down but giving one last burst of hot light before it moves away for the day. Into another time zone. For other people. But I'm not concerned much about other people. Other time zones. Not now. Not today. Not lately. All there is and needs to be is this small world in the garden city. My wife with her feet in the kiddie pool. Our kids running through the sprinkler. Their fingers, lips, and tongues stained blue and red from eating superhero Popsicles.

We'll pray for rain tonight. After the kids have gone to bed. And I hope it comes fast and long and hard. Even if that means I cannot sleep. That tomorrow will be hotter and muggier. And that I'll be in this same chair. Smack dab in the middle of the same routine. Sweating. Drinking ice water. Saying the same things.

Because sometimes, all we need is a break.

A change of temperature.

Drops of rain.

It would be a fine night for a downpour. For me and S.B. to sit on the front porch, under the ugly awning. Breathing deeply. Saying nothing. And smiling. But we won't do that if it does not rain. Instead, we'll sit on the couch or lay in bed, crank up the fans, and watch a movie. Escape a little into the night. The dark. Away from the sun. And we'll try to edge close to sleep. So that our pillows will take us deep. To places we cannot now be. In this heat. This city. In this time zone. With all this love steeped in responsibility and expectation.

"If I didn't have kids, I'd live in the heart of a big city," said S.B.

She swirled her feet in the water of the small yellow pool.

"If I didn't have kids, I'd live in the country," I said.

I stepped into the pool. Stood in the water. Relief shot up my legs, into my gut, through my arms.

S.B. smiled.

"You are a country bumpkin at heart," she said.

I sat down in the pool. Looked over at the kids. Our daughter, a few weeks away from being one. Our son, four and going on twenty. Both of them smiling. Laughing. Wet and new and innocent in the green grass, the cold water, the fading daylight. And I knew that our talk meant nothing. It was only the talk of tired parents. A husband and wife that don't have time for dates, quiet dinners, or sex. And watching the kids, I knew that we could not want it any other way.

"We need a vacation," I said.

"We do," said S.B. "Some place warm."

I splashed her.

"It's plenty warm," I said.

"Warm, not hot," she said, and she splashed me back.

"Some place by the water. An ocean. A lake. I don't care. Just you and me and a cabin. Sleeping in and staying up late and walking the beach and swimming and ..."

Just then, our daughter took her brother's Popsicle and he threw himself to the ground.

"They're beat," said S.B.

"Yes. Fun in the sun. Sweet treats. All that running."

And we got up. Shared a look that we used to share before we were WE and the kids were our kids and life took off running, and I knew that one day we would have it again. Just like we did when I would visit her in the city and when she would drive out to see me in the country. But for now, there were more important things to carry.

"I'll get her," she said.

"I'll get him," I said.

And each of us carried a wet, sticky, crying kid inside. Out of the sun. Out of the heat. Away from the end of another good day in our garden in the city.

try and try again

Got a copy of THE SUN in the mail. Tried to read it. Twice. Once the night before last. Unable to sleep. Wide awake and alert. But nothing took. Couldn't get into the words. Find meaning. Feel the gut. And so, I set it aside. It *was* late. I *must* have been tired. I'm sure I'd used up my brain power for the day.

I gave it another crack tonight. Feeling good and upbeat. Wanting nothing more than to read something—anything—that could hit the sweet spot; I settled into the sofa under the soft light of the lamp and readied myself for the hook. The bait. The language that would resonate. Take me away to another place. At least for a page. But there was nothing.

But that's not Sy's fault. And it's not the fault of the writers. It's my fault. I'd rather write than read. Create than believe. And in the whole scheme of things, there are plenty of people that do not like my writing. For example, THE SUN. I must have received at least half a dozen rejection letters from Sy and the boys over the past ten years. And now, I know why. My writing is not a good fit. Has not hit the mark. Is exactly what they are not looking for. And that's fine. There are plenty of magazines publishing writers that are worse than me. So I have hope.

And besides, I've got bigger fish to fry.

I moved Friday's wine to Thursday. Am nearing the bottom of the glass. And feeling good. I got burps out of my daughter, read a story to my son, and I got each of them to bed. I fed cat food to the dogs. Dog food to the cats. And I put them to bed too. I exercised thirty minutes so hard that sweat filled my eyes and my muscles begged for rest. And by God, I got see my wife naked for ten seconds, as I talked to her through the half-open bathroom door. She was just out of the shower. Fresh and smooth and more gorgeous than I remember. And now, I can't remember anything she said. Something about the kids, or my dentist appointment, or conditioner. Yes, that was it! Conditioner! She was in the shower, thinking about everything that knocks her silly every day and she filled her hands with conditioner and started washing her body. Oh, that glorious body! But of course, that's not what conditioner is for and her lapse in thinking, as I can attest, is directly related to the amount of time my daughter and son spend whining and crying and clinging to her legs.

But I digress, and I'm trying to forget and wind down from the day, so I'm onto that wine. A dirt cheap bottle of Bay Bridge Cabernet Sauvignon that will likely see it's end tonight because I'm feeling cocky and strong and much too alert for a hot and muggy Thursday night in the city. And really, what else is there to do?

All we ever really have are moments. Some of them alone. Most of them not. And the only thing we can ever do is our best. Hold doors open for strangers and friends. Say please, thank you, excuse me. Don't talk with a mouthful. Admit our mistakes. And always give people the benefit of the doubt. Common courtesy and a willingness to do right by others can take you to high places in this world. But that's old school. The blue-collar way. And with so many people full of shit, with their bad stories, bad attitudes, ignorant, selfish ways, having forgiveness and patience is hard to do.

But because of my wife and kids, our family—the part of the world we've made our own—I am hopeful. Have faith. And I believe that what we create is the basis of BIG, lasting Truth.

Like my wife's kiss.

Son's smile.

Daughter's blue eyes.

And the power of the gut. The place that knows and fights and loves without fear. Because it's important to try and try again. To care deeply. Accept blame. And keep on keepin' on. Even when there is no hook. No bait. And the language does not resonate. When there is no other place, but here. At the end of the page. And you are left with nothing.

a world awake and moving

Sunday morning up and running. And all sounding as it should. Quiet and still, except for the bird calling from the big Silver Maple outside the window. I know the bird, its call, but it is too early to find the information. To remember its name. Synapses are just warming up. Coffee has not yet blasted the bloodstream. And so, I'll not force myself to a standstill trying to remember the bird.

There is little traffic on Merriman. No jets powering through the sky. And so right now, I could be just about anywhere. Writing from a cabin up north. The beach in Saint Thomas. Or a rinky-dink motel in Pinconning. That's the beauty of early morning. When the world is asleep, the sun is slowly rising, and hopes and dreams are as real as mortgage payments, utility bills, and making ends meet.

Short this week. On sleep and money. But all filled up on patience and ambition. So there is a strange balance. Even a little more happiness than usual. I'm not sure why. My four year old son keeps using his bedroom as a bathroom. My eleven month old daughter has already learned the art of high-pitched, shrieking tantrums, and my wife is in need of a vacation. From the kids. The house. From me. I would like to pack her up. Drive her to the airport. Send her on her way.

"See you next week, honey!"

I would say this to her as I hand her the credit card.

"But where am I going?" she'd ask.

"Anywhere you want. That's the beauty of it!"

"But what about you and the kids? Who will watch them while you're at work? Who will do laundry and dishes? Clean up pee and poop? Cook?"

"We'll figure it out."

Because we would. People who care and love and make vows and have respect for themselves and those around them—these people—they figure it out. They do what's necessary. They make sacrifices. Satisfy needs that are not their own. Just as my wife does each and every day with little complaint. Never asking or expecting a thing. And so, I try to give a little here and there. A foot rub. Shoulder massage. Pitching in where I can to make her life easier. But still, it is not enough. She needs a vacation. And this would be her big chance. Her time to fly. To be free from the roles of

Mommy and Wife. To see more than the walls and floors of our small house. To get away from our lower-middle class life in the city. To be alone. At peace. To roam.

She would look at the credit card in her hand. Shift nervously— back and forth—on the heels of her feet. Bury herself in guilt. Feel bad about having fun. Feel bad about taking a trip. Getting away. Feel horrible about spending money.

"But where should I go?"

"Anywhere that doesn't require a passport, I guess."

We would hug and kiss. Begin to miss the comfort of each other. But we would be all right. No matter where we are, apart or together, I know we'll be all right. And so, I'd watch with pride as my beautiful, brave wife started toward her destination.

"Oh, wait!" I would call after her. "Try not to spend over $3500 bucks. That's all that's left on the card!"

She would roll her eyes. Consider scrapping the whole trip. But I would high-tail it out of there. Leaving her on the edge of a liberating experience. Knowing full-well she would not pay the twenty bucks for a cab ride back home. She would have no choice but to move ahead. Show the world her strength. And have fun.

Marriage is like that sometimes. You want to lock the kids in their rooms. Ship your spouse to Zimbabwe. Or take off on your own. Even if only for a day. To rent a hotel room. Lay in bed. And sleep. Breathe and stretch and get back that part of you that gets buried and sometimes lost as you fulfill your roles, obligations, and meet the expectations of everyone else every day. But, more often than not, marriage is the truest experience a man can have.

It keeps me honest. On the right path. And it keeps me here. A million miles away, steeped in thought and words, but only a few feet from the place my family sleeps. Where my dedication lies. And as long as I have this—these Sunday morning bouts of perspective that drive me to do nothing but the best for the best people I'll ever know—I'll be all right. And to be all right in this life is more than I deserve and more than I could ever ask for.

Up and running. And all is sounding as it should. Traffic has picked up on Merriman. People are driving to breakfast, to work, to church. And the birds—blue jays, sparrows, cardinals, and robins— are calling from the trees. The Silver Maple, the Cottonwood, the Hickory. Synapses are firing like mad. Coffee is coursing the bloodstream. And it is time to go inside. Make the big Sunday breakfast. Kiss my wife. Hug my kids. Get back to this good life we have. Another chance. Another morning. A world awake and moving.

self-centered shots at peace of mind

Little Penguin tells me to pony up. Sack up. Do whatever it takes to get the MFA. To get the terminal degree so that I can show people I've accomplished something. But Little Penguin is fired up. Fueled by half his bottle. And penguins don't know much about being a man. A Hubby. A Daddy. So I have half a mind to slug down the rest of Mr. Penguin, pack my bags, and move north. Away from this city. Away from this limbo. And write. Only write. I would strip away the fat. Unload things and belongings. I would grow my own vegetables. Hunt for meat. Fish for fish. And I would write the best goddamned stories that I could write. But a man cannot move his family on a whim. He cannot pay bills with hope. And my wife and kids cannot live on words. Especially mine. These self-centered shots at peace of mind.

Tomorrow, we will load the car. Luggage. People. Dogs. And we will turn a 250 mile trip into a whole day's drive. Because bladders cannot synch. Kids cannot wait. And S.B. and I will need a break. From the hum of tires on pavement. Kids whining in the backseat. And everything that waits.

Uncertainty.

Chance.

A shot in the dark.

"What if they offer you less than you're making?" she says.

"I'll take it."

"But what about the bills?"

"Fuck the bills."

She is silent. We are at the bonfire. It is tonight. Not tomorrow. And so there is nothing but the falling of night, the flicker of flame, and fireflies.

"I don't want us to move if we are going to struggle," she says.

"Honey, we'll always struggle."

I say this, but I know it is not true. If anything, it will always be me. The struggler. Pushing. Shoving. Digging deep. Trying to make the difference. So that kids can grow and love and trust. So my wife can sleep soundly. Paint pictures. Be free in sweet dreams.

"But why? Why would we?" she asks.

I want to tell her that the struggle, the failure, the life of trying and trying again is in my blood. Part of me. That it is the reason I wake, walk, live and breathe, but I cannot. So, we are silent at the fire. My mind wanders. And I know that the only thing that can save us is if I have a drink.

Little Penguin tells me to pony up. Make good. Do what it takes to get the MFA. Because good is good. All days are steeped in haphazard regret. And each of us is an important piece. Hunting for meat. Fishing for fish. And paying bills with hope. The thing with feathers. That feeds and breeds and flies. And takes with it these crummy words, these self-centered shots at peace of mind.

wanting nothing else

When the world gets too serious—when my wife and I cannot meet in the middle, when it's too goddamned hot, and when everything has beaten me down—I like sit at these keys and write it all away. Marriage. Family. Job. The dogs. The cats. The house. The cars. I like to write all of it away, so that I am disconnected, separated, gone away to the empty place. Where there is nothing but me and relaxation and words.

But a man is not supposed to think like this. To want to leave. Escape. Get away. He should always want to be loving his wife and his kids. Hugging them. Kissing them. Doing everything for them. A man should not think of himself. He should not think of being alone. A man should not want to be only a man.

He should want things.

He should feel a deep desire to fulfill roles.

Meet expectations.

Be Hubby.

Daddy.

Handyman.

And he should not want sex twice a week. Blow jobs once a month. And he should not want to go fishing, or spend time with friends. He should not want anything but to be exactly what he believed he would be five minutes before he took his vows.

And if he does want any of these things, he should not speak of them. He should not share them. He should not write about them and think about them and have them run their course via the safety of ink and drink and pen.

It's hot. Muggy. Another irritable fucking night in the city.

All I want to do is sleep alone in a tub of cool water. But men drown in tubs late at night. And there's nothing that can take away this heat. Nothing. And so, I'll just get through it. Like I get through everything. And I'll keep my chin up knowing that tomorrow is a new day. Another chance. And odds are pretty good that I'll be alive. Able to say, "Goodbye, I love you," to my wife. And shower and dress and head off to work.

An air conditioned office in an affluent part of town.

Another keyboard.

A screen.

But my mind wrapped up in words that do not—and never can—belong to me because they were written by people smarter and brighter and richer. People that somehow have figured out the route to doing what they love. Even if it is something that nobody else loves or understands.

Like being a man. Tired and stressed. Wanting nothing but everything that waits in sleep and dream.

the next best thing

The day winding down and it feels like it was bigger and more important and more beautiful and more exhausting than it was. And for some reason I feel have I have the push to put me up over the edge. Into the place we need to be. Slow. Steady. Sure. An old, weary prize-fighter feeding his family blow by blow. The farm hand picking rocks in hundred degree heat to pay off what he owes. The aging writer. Hung up on what might have been. But living well in this new territory where nights are no longer spent in dark bars. With pretty girls in black dresses. Planning the next best thing.

These days, I'm onto other things. Making up for mistakes. Making good on promises. Upholding vows. Doing what I can to right wrongs—most of them not even mine—so that my daughter can laugh. My son can play. And my wife can sleep soundly and dream.

It is a big life full of big days. But it's hard to keep perspective. To stay afloat. When some days all I want to do is slip down and out. Drink for days. Read books I've already read. Then read them again.

Attwood rolling around naked in mud, surfacing only by way of her roots. O'Connor flavoring the every day with dark happenstance. Amanda Davis circling the drain. And when I've sobered up or drank myself into a steady rut of regret, I'd like to write the best fucking story that's ever been.

They say it can't be done.

But most of what they say is bullshit. And they are too far gone anyway to ever understand where it comes from. And most everything everyone says about nothing being original and everything already being done is not true.

It is coming. Making its way through dark veins. Up from the gut. Pushed by the big red muscle that's been the only thing that has ever made a difference in anything—music, writing, art—and all of the sudden I'm on it. In it. Deep and hard. And there's not a goddamned thing I can do, but keep on keepin' on.

Start all over again. As the day winds down. Sounds settle. And I think of my family. My wife. All of us together in this big life. And I know that I must not be afraid to push. To get us over this edge. Into the place we need to be. Strong. Steady. Sure. Willing to swing hard and follow through. To work the earth. Dig deep into these words. And look forward to what's to come. Our small life. In this new place. Far from the dark. Ready to rise up. Make it. The next best thing to be done.

living well

Even the city is pretty in the morning. Out first thing to get sausage and eggs. Orange juice and the paper. Me and Jovi. Our big trip together. Half mile away. To Kroger. Her strapped into her baby seat. Me in the driver's seat, but already 250 miles away. Imagining us—all of us—in the car headed to Lake Huron. The beach. With a picnic packed. Towels, suntan lotion, and inflatable water toys. To spend a slow summer day together. In sun and water. Far away from this city where noise never stops and the only peace I ever feel is like the peace we had this morning. Going to the grocery store. Little traffic. A snail's pace. And aisles and checkout lanes clear to make for easy shopping.

I've had enough of jets ruining the sky. Enough of disrespectful people demanding respect. And I've had enough of this garden on the outskirts of the big city. Each of them dying a little more each day. Boarded up buildings. Houses stripped clean. People too lazy to walk their garbage to the trash can. Lives stymied by limbo. A world giving up on its own.

I know there will always be some of this. That some people don't care about rising, exceeding expectations, doing what's right. There will be people up north just as lazy and disrespectful and caught up in struggles of their own making. But I also know that roots run much deeper up north. That people are strong by way of hard work, will, and having their feet firmly planted in the earth. And I know that it is the best place to raise our kids. Strengthen our vows. And live well.

And living well is all any of us ever want.

It's not big paychecks. Having stuff.

It is short, quiet trips to the grocery store. First thing in the morning. So that you can buy sausage and eggs. Orange juice and the newspaper. It is pushing your daughter in the grocery cart. Listening to her ooooh and aaaah at bright packaging, and it is feeling good because you know that the two of you will be home in a matter of minutes. To see your wife and son and begin another day. To rise. Exceed expectations. And take the steps necessary to plant our feet firmly in the earth.

Tomorrow she'll be one. Already, she has given us a lifetime. What they say about kids and marriage and parenting and love—all of it—is true. It is the hardest work you will ever do. It is not for those seeking instant gratification. It is not for those unwilling to give more than they have. It is not for those that need constant applause. Family life—good family life—is not for the weak or for the selfish. Family life, I think, is for those of us seeking more. Call it God. Call it "making it." Call it hitting the sweet spot. Call it Truth. Whatever it is, you cannot know it until you are in the thick of it. Smack dab in the middle of shitty diapers, tantrums, saying hurtful things to your wife. And struggling to make ends meet. Those times—the ones when you want to cut ties, say fuck it, and leave—those are the ones that test the gut. Punch you with perspective. Kick you square in the nuts and make you, somehow, want more.

And goddammit, I want more.

I want two hundred more of my daughter's birthdays. I want a million more fishing trips with my son. I want to hug my wife until my arms work no more. But I know better. And I know what waits.

It is not a happy ending. It is not where I'll want to be.

But fading to black is something we practice at the end of each day. And so tonight, I'll think long and hard about the end. Finishing up. Giving way to whatever else comes. Everything or nothing. A bright light or constant dream. And I'll know that if I die in a car wreck tomorrow, everything is as beautiful and true as it should be.

But there'll be no wrecking.

Like Amanda Davis in a plane.

Plath and the oven.

Hemingway cleaning his shotgun.

I'm not good enough for that. And I don't want to be.

If I had my choice, I'd always be not good enough and write sentences too plain to make good stories if it meant I'd never die. That tomorrow would always come.

Because my daughter turns one tomorrow. My son is itching to go fishing. And watching my wife makes me realize I've married up. That I'm in a better place than I deserve. And that even though we

103

are only pilgrims keeping at the keepin' on, what we are doing is important and big and lasting. And when it is time to turn the final page, we will be satisfied with what we've done.

Up and into another hot muggy day. Sick of the heat. The stickiness. Tired from being tired all the time. But soon, this will pass. One week and counting and we'll be unpacking boxes. Opening windows. Airing out our new home in the place we were born. Grew up. And raised.

I'm looking forward to the move. To being back in a place where people have deep roots. Not because of color or religion or lifestyle, but because of place. The big lake. The winding river. The inland lakes, streams, and creeks. A place where people are not ashamed to hunt their meat, catch their fish, pick their own fruits and vegetables. A place bound by a close-knit, easy-going nature. Where people take care of their own. Look out for each other. Are unafraid to lend a helping hand.

Thugs and thieves. Child molesters and wife beaters. They don't last long up there. They are run out of town. Found face down and bloated in cold water. Or they are never found at all. It does not take much to make a bad man disappear. It is done quietly. In the thick of night. Or under the wide blue skies that span the inland sea. And if you are a bad man in this place, you can be sure your days are numbered. That you'll not last. That somehow the good will get you.

Because every day is a good day to fight the good fight. To do what's right. Even if that means a good man must sometimes be bad.

But enough of all that. It is too early in the day to wander so near the dark. And those that run in the dark, day after day, they know the light is coming.

What I need now—more than ever—is an hour that runs into another that runs into another so that I can get back at it. I've been away too long. Jake and Kali. Tom and Shelley. Aden, his Pilgrim's Bay, and all he hopes it will be. I need to get back into that ratty old booth. Drink pitcher after pitcher. And talk with them about fishing and fucking and fighting and God. I need to feel the pull of the hollow. Rise up from the bottom and show them how good it can be if we are true, honest, and fearless in the face of brutality. The broken dreams. Empty promises. Skeletons and memories that

105

linger in the deep. I need to show them that there is hope not only in the thing with feathers, but everywhere.

In fact. Fiction. In words and punches and broken windows and blood. Always in blood. And if we are able to make the hard decisions. Carry the ones we love. And keep at this keepin' on, there is nothing but glory. Subtle, silent glory. A life of small victories. Won inch by inch. Minute by minute. Day by day. By creating a Code. Memorizing it. Acting on it. And never being afraid of being alone.

And so, let's step on into it. Another hot and muggy one. All of us tired and sick of this heat. But hopeful. And aware that soon, this will pass. One week left. And counting. Then we'll be unpacking. Breathing fresh air through open windows. Ready to grow. Be raised. And born again.

finding home

Up at six this morning. Doing this for me. For the words. For whatever it is that drives me back to these keys. And I find that the spiral bound notebook that my son's been using for coloring, scribbling, and smacking his sister is one I used in 2006. _Central Michigan University_, it says on the cover. And written on the front inside page, _English 460_. There is some irony, fate, magic in this— that my son is scribbling the shit out of one of my old college notebooks—but it's too early to go deep and so I do what any other Dad would do. I pick it up. Thumb through pages and pages of my son's thoughts and feelings. And I'm amazed. He's pretty good at drawing faces. On one page, there are four ghost-like figures that by body size and shape are dead giveaways. He has drawn our family. Each of us with a different expression. His short round sister is happily confused. His mother is nearly cross-eyed and frowning. I have the serious, straight face. And my boy, he is nearly upside down on the page with a big smile plastered across his face. I suppose this is a fair representation of us most days.

My daughter may not be completely confused, but she floats around here like she's a visitor from another planet. A happy one analyzing and absorbing every detail so she can provide a full report when she returns to the Mothership. My wife—I've seen her cross-eyed and frowning, that's for sure. Usually on Thursdays at 5:10 pm when I walk in the door. Four days down. One to go. And the kids have her on the ropes. One day, I'm afraid I'll come home and the house will be ripped to shreds. The kids will be screaming, toilets overflowing, smoke alarms beeping, and I'll find my wife locked in the closet. Rocking back-and-forth, sucking her thumb. Not because she doesn't know what she's doing. My wife is more capable and strong than anyone I know. But because being at home—day after day with two little kids—is exhausting. Especially when one of them is fearless, knows everything, and can turn the world upside down in a heartbeat—and do it smiling, of course.

Ours is a good life. We've got it made. We could have more stuff, more money, more shit we don't need, but we've got plenty already. A few years ago, when S.B. and I realized we were knee-deep in each other and that there was no turning back, we came to an agreement.

Have fun. Be thankful. Live simply.

And by Christ, it's working. We've had some bare bone times trying to make ends meet. We've had our share of ups and downs and limbo just like everyone else. But we've decided that slow and steady does win the race. And even though we're not celebrating our small victories with champagne and caviar, we have discovered that a cheap box of wine, Triscuits and some cheese can be just as good. Especially when you have tasted the bottom. When you know what it's like to have not.

There is nothing like finding home. Knowing that you are surrounded by people that love you. And knowing that despite all your failures in the past you are on the right path.

The sky is orange over the big lake this morning. Promising another beautiful day. I'm drinking coffee. Having fun. Thankful that we are alive and well. Thankful that such a simple life can be so fulfilling. And thankful that I am here—on the sunrise side—up early. Doing this for me. For the words. For whatever it is that drives me back to these keys. And it is exactly as I had hoped. Even better. Being back North. In the place I was born and raised. In the place that gave me my wife. In the place I've laid roots. And this, I now know, is where the story begins.

It's the ringing in my ears. *Greetings From Cutler County.* Wanting to do more than make ends meet. Michael Van Walleghen. The Jesse Besser Museum. And it's the third glass of wine. And I find that no matter how many days rise and fall and build up under my belt, I'm the same kid I was when I lived on The Ridge. Packed full of hope. Aimed at Truth. Fighting the good fight even though I knew I'd lose.

Because we all do. There's no getting around that.

Ask the President of ACI. My realtor. The five-year old boy that fell into an open septic tank and drowned. Died in shit and piss and fear. Ask anyone who has lived enough to see people die and you'll come to know that there isn't much more than the moment.

This.

And I wonder how *this* ever started at all. A boy stuck inside himself. A man trying to figure shit out. Another body struggling within the constraints of heart and mind. Wanting nothing but to eat, drink, fuck and have fun, but be overwhelmed with all the stitches and blooms and responsibilities that come when a man is tired of being alone.

Back in the day, my Grandpa Stevens shot two deer at once. Leaned over the backside of a Chevy Impala. Nine beers into the evening. Open sights. Across a driveway, scrub brush, the railroad tracks, and a field. With a lever-action .30/.30 Winchester. Over 100 yards away. Into one deer and out another. My Dad was there. Witnessed it all. Told me this story at least twice. Maybe more. I was younger then. More impressionable. But if he told it to me now, 10:56 pm on a Thursday night, 2010, I'd believe it even more.

Because men are different now. They don't hunt. They don't drink to keep straight. And they don't shoot off-hand through open sights with a bottle of Pfeiffer's tucked in their back pocket to fill the freezer so their kids can eat.

Instead, we are weak.

Soft hands. Nice clothes. Full of shit and big ideas and all sorts of things that this world does not need. Has never needed. And I think it takes a lot to make a man realize what's important and lasting, that at the center of things there is an aching silence that guides and protects and makes us strong. That life can be summarized in something as simple and beautiful as a tall, lean steelworker wringing his big hands around a shot of muzzle-flash.

"We were happy that he got us something to eat."

That's what my Dad said.

"But that shot? Who does those things?" I asked.

"Men that wanted to feed their families," he said.

I sit—at this moment—in a nice house in a good spot, in a place close enough to Lake Huron that I can hear waves bursting on the shore. In a room. At a computer. Drinking Merlot. There is a beautiful built-in gun cabinet to my right. And it is empty.

But I am full up on ringing. Lineage. Books that aren't that good. And I know for a goddamned fact that because of all the things that have happened in the past, we are fighters. Aimed at Truth. And that it does not matter if we win or lose.

many dimensions of love

I want to write about a time in my Saint Paul days. When I was not yet 30. Thought I had the world by the balls. When I was sure that I'd be somebody. That I could do or say anything because for me, the rules did not apply. I want to slip into that booth. Hold that 32 ounce mug of Leinenkugel Honey Weiss. Hear Lunde and J.C., the music, the conversation. I want to smell the smoke. Taste the air and know all I knew then.

Which was nothing. But nothing meant everything and emptiness made me full. And when you set out to creatively deconstruct your life from ground to sky and back again, nothing and the hollow space it creates can be the most valuable thing you'll ever find.

But that's me. Or it used it be. And that was my Code. Tear it all down. Past the walls and studs. Past the foundation. Through the septic, below the drain field, and deep to where it begins. In the dark, most basic elements. Good and evil and the many dimensions of love.

It was in one of those booths, in one of those bars, that I once told J.C.—a single mother of a four year old boy—that a person could never have success in life if they chose parenting over passion. I was humming with alcohol. Teetering on that edge where everything feels like an epiphany.

"I don't want to marry or have kids or do any of that shit we're supposed to do," I said.

J.C. sipped her beer. Lunde chuckled. As usual, they let me continue. Dig myself deeper. Bury myself with my own shovel.

"People that marry and get sucked into fulfilling the roles of mother and father, hubby and wife—they spend their lives getting dumber and fatter while the world keeps trucking on. We aren't meant to sit and settle. We are meant for greater things."

Lunde leaned back and smiled. As usual, he was along for the ride. Helping me reach great heights by letting me plummet to the bottom.

J.C. adjusted her shirt, tugged at her shorts. She was growing increasingly uncomfortable.

"I think you're wrong, K.J.," she said.

I waited. Polished off my mug. Held it up as the waitress passed so I could get another. J.C.'s cheeks went pink. She bit her lip as she took off her glasses.

"No I'm not wrong, J.C."

"Yes, you are. You make it sound like all anyone should ever do is what they want to do, but that's not how it works."

"You say that because you have a kid," I said.

"Of course, that's why I say that! I love my boy!"

"And you should, and you're a great Mom, and that's all fine and dandy, but what I'm saying is this—people make choices. They pour into their passion or they pour into their family. You are either a hell of a parent or really fucking good at something. You can't be both."

"That's absurd," she said. "You're talking out of your ass."

I laughed. It was good to see J.C. jacked up this way. Twisted up in knots. But I was firm in my stance. I had seen her with her son. I had met him. He was a beautiful kid. Well-behaved. Fun. Respected his Mom. But J.C. would never be a great, successful painter, or writer, or musician. She would not be a great quilter, bowler, or chef. She would never really be great at anything—not to the point it would support her family and maintain balance and harmony.

"It's just not possible," I said.

Lunde leaned forward. Tapped his empty mug on the table.

"Another round," he said. "And let's do some shots."

And I'm sure we did. And the conversation moved on. And J.C. and Lunde may have forgotten that night. But I have not. Because now, I'm everything I never expected to be.

Pushing 40. Married. Two kids. Living a small town life in the place me and my wife were born and raised. It is like a dream. This is not reality. It can't be. We have it good. We're doing well. We're healthy, comfortable, happy.

There is this—the ache, the itch, the writing—and now I can see that what I had said ten years ago was something, indeed, shot right out of my ass. J.C. was right. And in his casual silence, Lunde was right too. He let me wield that fucking shovel night after night. Again and again. Until I was so buried in my own self-centered bullshit, that there was nothing to do, but dig my way out.

And I have. It's taken years. Things are not the same as they were in those Saint Paul days. They can't be and never will be. And for that, I am glad.

And as my wife wrangles two screaming and crying kids into the house from playing outside on a chilly October Sunday, I know there are different measures of success. Many dimensions of love. Being a good parent and a solid husband is what helps. Not only here in our little world, but in the whole scheme of things as we push along, fighting the good fight, working to tip the scales so that good wins out over evil. So I keep the faith. Stay strong. And believe. So my wife and my kids know I still have gas in my tank. That I can and will do it all. Build great things. With a hammer and nails. Shovel and sweat. And that these words will last and keep us safe from the empty, hollow space inside.

shake up the comfort

Don't want to write about hunger or lack of sleep or desire because all these have ever done is make a man eat more, sleep less, and want things he cannot have. And so, this morning, we will pretend we have a full belly, that we logged seven hours of solid rest, and that there is nothing but what's between these four walls that I need to know.

I've picked and eaten enough fruit directly from the tree to see that there's more. That things can be better. But I also know that once you start, it's hard to stop. And spending a life at low hanging branches does nothing but make you soft and lazy, and this world is filling up with the soft and the lazy, so I am up and at it. Forcing the plugs to fire. Working to set the idle. Unsure of what the day will bring but unafraid to give it another try.

Because that's what you do when you know time is running out. When you know that each word to word to sentence to sentence is a string of moments you cannot get back. And your only hope of lasting long enough to make a difference in this small world is to keep doing what you love. Sharing what you're good at. Even if it falls on deaf ears.

But I don't believe we're all deaf. It's just a matter of people caring enough to tune in. And if you care about what you do, others care about what you do. And so, the ears open. The eyes widen and there is a strange, familiar moment of recognition.

"It's like I've been here before," I said to S.B. two nights ago, as we sat together in bed.

"This movie we're watching, the lighting of the room, us here in bed—EVERYTHING—I'm sure this has happened before."

"Déjà-vu," she said.

"But it's strange. It's been about two minutes of déjà-vu."

"Maybe we've been here before," she said as she moved closer and squeezed my hand.

"That's gotta be it," I said. And my mind ticked and pulled and begged me to think, to dig deeper for more lasting recognition, as if I was on the edge of an old familiar dream. But I didn't want to go. To leave the warm bed, my wife, that moment that coincided with some parallel world, a life I may have lived before, and so I stayed. And here I remain.

I don't want to go to someplace I've been. To start over again. We've come too far for that. There are stories to write. There's work to be done. There is S.B. and the little ones to love. And I gotta buck up. Shake up the comfort. Do what it takes to push myself higher. Away from this low hanging fruit. Through the field, into the water, up the giant hill that leads beyond the ridge and into the forest. Where it is dark and cold and you must use your senses to navigate through sinkholes, thickets, and deadfalls that know no time and do not care if you make it out alive.

Because that's where I'll find what we need. To eat less. Sleep more. To believe to the core that there's no place like home. Pushing ahead is better than living in the past. Taking control of your own destiny is better than waiting for the path. And so, I am up and at it. Forcing the plugs to fire. Working to set the idle. Unsure of what the day will bring, but unafraid to give it another try.

art of happy distraction

It's never too late to change. Shake it up. Rise from what you've known and try something different. Change is good. Keeps us fresh. Makes us appreciate what we've had. Makes us want more. For our wives and kids. For us. Because even though nothing really matters, it is the art of happy distraction that makes life what it is. A series of moments tied together by the development of personal relationships.

You get better at everything as you grow. Fighting, thinking, writing, and believing. You get better at patience and listening and following through. No longer is it swing and swing and swing with fury and force. Now, it is swing, wait for it, and follow through. Connect with precision. Swing less, but hit the mark more.

And that's where we are this morning. The end of a work week. The beginning of a weekend. Little boxes on a calendar. Checking them off. One at a time. As we push through day after day, week after week, working through these little daily battles that mean nothing, but everything.

It is walking home from work and seeing my wife and kids coming down the sidewalk to meet me.

The four year old son … _DADDY! DADDY!_ His big smile. His arms and legs pumping like crazy as he runs to me.

The fourteen month old girl … _DAAAH-DAAAH! DAAAH-DAAAH!_ Walking as fast as she can, waving.

And my wife. Walking behind them. Her slow, easy gait. Curly locks bouncing. And always—no matter what the weather—the sun shining all around her.

This is what drives me. Keeps me coming and keeps me going.

There are not many things in a man's life that make a difference, but there are many things. And if you have enough of them in your life that make an impact, that hit the gut and stick, you can be sure that when the big things do come—marriage and family—you will pay attention. Make sacrifices. Do whatever it takes to make IT work.

It is never too late to change. Not even now … 37 years into a life I've lived shaken. Stirred. From a glass. A mug. And straight from the bottle. It is important to rise. Shake the dust off what I've known, read it again, and write something new. Because change is good. The movement and unknown—they keep us fresh. Make us appreciate what we've had and want more.

Of our wives.

Our kids.

And us.

Because even though nothing really matters, it is the art of happy distraction that makes life what it is. And so, we rise. Take the first steps of this Saturday morning. And we do it all again.

things worth knowing

Snow in the sky. Wide gray clouds moving North to South. Soon, the flakes will be coming to stay for good. That means the snowblower's tires and shear pins need to be fixed. That I need to invest in one serious snow shovel. That I need to give the cars a final oil change and a look-see before we start pushing them through the cold, the salt, and the slush. There's wood to haul from The Ridge to 2nd Avenue. And in my head, I have silly wintertime dreams. Me and my four-year old boy. Thermoses full of hot cocoa. Driving the back roads in a four-wheel-drive truck. Road-tackling tires. Heavy duty suspension. Outfitted with a plow. Busting through drifts, climbing hills. Keeping our eyes peeled for cars and trucks that have been eaten up by the snow. Me and my boy, stopping at Mia and Peepa's to plow their driveway. Then back into town plow Nana and Papa's. Me and my boy, thrilled with our efforts. Man and machine versus Mother Nature. The woman that always wins, but lets us pretend we are champs by winning small battles.

"This is fun!" he will shout, as we shove another mountain of snow out of our way.

"It sure is!" I'll chime.

And we will bop along to early doses of Christmas music, level out with David Gray, and rise again with Pearl Jam.

But I dream a lot. And hardly any of them ever come true. I've always wanted silly stupid things. Distractions—big and small—to keep me from giving up and losing my mind. It used to be that this time of year was for deer. Scouting the small parcel in The Ridge for rubs and scrapes. Droppings and trails. Plugging holes and cracks in the old outhouse turned deer blind. Preparing for two weeks of cold and waiting. Waiting and cold. So that I could watch the sun rise and light the frozen world. See chickadees, squirrels, and jays scatter snow from cedar trees. And so I could listen to sounds only the woods can make. Hunting, although I was never really good at it, made me happy. It was never about the kill—no man in his right mind enjoys killing anything—but it was about being there, where so many other men had been before. In the cold and waiting. Mulling thoughts and scenarios over and over in my mind. Breathing *that* air. Wondering if they were the same thoughts, scenarios, and breaths my Dad and Grandpa, and all men before them, once had.

I haven't hunted in five years. I know that it's something we grow out of. That sooner or later that part of us dies a little. But there are things I want to hold onto. Things that I love—like hunting and fishing and camping and driving trucks through back roads—that make me a better listener, more patient—a better man. There are people that cannot understand this. That don't believe it. But that's okay because I do. And I am the one behind the wheel. Taking aim. Threading hooks. Making fires. Clearing drives. And these are the things I want to pass on—not because *I* have done them and loved them—but because they are worth knowing, and there is deep satisfaction in eating food you've worked for. Warming your family with a fire that's fed by wood you've split and carried. And knowing that they will be able to walk freely on paths you've worked so hard to keep clear.

But this isn't about hunting, fishing, cutting wood, or any of those things. It's about all of them. And getting older and feeling that even though I'm back where I belong—up north—I have lost touch with all the things that made me love this place so much. And it's a shame because I'm not done. There is *more* to all of this—my up north existence. And even though my life as Hubby and Daddy come first, I need the dreaming and doing. The silly, boyish distractions. Wintertime or not. Snow or sunshine. If I'm to be balanced and happy, if I'm to keep at this keepin' on, and put life into writing, then I need to remember that I'm the one at the keys. Pounding out this story. That even though the sun has come around now and plowed away the wide gray clouds, there is snow in that sky, and soon it will be coming to stay for good.

Packing on pounds, but feeling all right. There's never been anything heavy enough to weigh me down and keep me there. Most of my falling has been my own doing. I have always known this. And more often than not, I've created my own pitfalls and fuck ups. There's no getting around that. Any man that blames anybody else for the way he has or has not turned out gets what he deserves. And usually what he gets is a life of petty battles that do not matter because they cannot be won anyway. And so, as I drink a bit of wine and winter threatens to leave us all cold and dead for good, I am warm and happy. In the best place I've ever been. Steeped in reality. On the edge of something great. Simmering in the sweet sauces of home.

There is not much that can set me off. Steer me away. Take me off track. I've had an easy life made hard by my own mistakes. But not one of those mistakes was ever driven by ill intention. I have always believed I was meant for greater things. And as self-centered and egotistical as that sounds, I still believe it now.

Holt once told me that I was not meant for anything. I was not special, she said. I was not a pretty snowflake, a falling leaf. I was not a writer, a fighter, a friend. I was not anyone to believe in. I would never be anything to anyone because all I cared about was me, me, me.

So, I smiled and finished my drink. Tipped the waitress. Hugged Lunde. And I left. It was a cold Saint Paul night. I was a little lonely, but I knew that all I ever had to do was call somebody. Anybody, and it would be okay. And because I knew that, I never did. I kept drinking that night. Drove myself straight to the darkest place a man can get without being dark forever, and when I came up for air I found myself sitting on the edge of my bed. Bloody face. Legs shaking. Fists cut and broken. And I knew I had done enough and I had done all I could and it was time to move on. I needed to write of this place, and back then I could never write about the place I was in. And I wanted to write about it. To write about everything. Unemployment to good money. Ruining a marriage. Breaking trust and teeth and noses. Making friendships that even today know not the boundaries of distance, mistakes, or time. Eating three AM omelets. Swallowing pills. Mastering shots. Drinking an inland lake's worth of Leinenkugel's beer. Lots and lots of bad. A little good. Just me—wrapped up in myself—fuck-stepping along in my own little world. Living a nightmarish, beautiful dream. Running headlong into the unknown. Wanting nothing for everyone but good.

And now, there is all of this. The being here. Comforted by quiet. Fueled by love that grows deeper every day. Feeling fine-tuned and confident because sometimes boys that find the bottom become men that find the top. And when you get up high to a place like this—living small but aware of the largest things—you see that everything has led to this. A late-night, box-wine moment when you're a little blubbed up, but clearer than the December night sky, and you know that the reason you are so strong—stronger than you were ten years ago—is because you have a wife. One that gets you. And because you have kids. Kids that need you. And there isn't anything else in the world.

Not lost friends. A shoddy past. Not anything, but packing on pounds and feeling all right because there is nothing heavy enough to weigh me down.

thanksgiving day, 2010

Nine yellow apples. Stubborn ones. Clinging to the tree in the backyard. With the hard winds today—coming from all sides— something will likely give way. If not the place where stem meets branch, then along a branch somewhere. At the weakest place. And there will be a break—something nobody will hear or care about while eating turkey and mashed potatoes with gravy and stuffing and yams—and an apple will fall. Thud to the cold wet ground and it will die.

But today—despite the gray—it is not about dying. It is about giving thanks. Reveling in the gift of life. Our certain good fortune. Family. Friends. Wives and kids. Pets too, I guess. But our old cat, Ted—the one that's been with me the longest—is out there in this mess, testing the last bit of sense he has. Stalking. Tomming. Doing whatever it is he believes he can still do out there in the neighborhood wild. And because I've been sober a week, and because this change of seasons has really got hold of me, I am worried. Not about Ted so much, but about everything.

A week ago, at two-thirty in the morning—winter howling and lapping at this old house—I could hear Ted yowling and crying. Yowling and crying. As if there was great danger. It was a sound I'd never heard him make before, but I knew it was Ted and that he needed help. And even though I have a wife and kids and dogs and cats, and I have been surrounded by love and care and kindness my whole life, I am not a caring man. So it was hard getting out of bed. Walking out into the icy night in my boxer shorts, a t-shirt, my sandals, and wandering the neighborhood to follow his sound. *He is broken up and stuck to the road*, I thought. *Or caught in a live trap.* But as I walked up 2nd Avenue then turned left onto Dunbar Street, I realized that the only danger that night would be if I was arrested for trespassing.

When I found him, I thought about leaving him there. But that vein of thought was soon lost. He knew I'd come to save him. He was pawing at the air. Whisking his tail. Happy to see me. And the noise—the awful, mournful sound—was so loud that I could not leave him there. Up high. On the roof of a house three lots down. If he kept it up, if I didn't get him down, he would wake someone. So, I took off my sandals. Embraced the cold winter air. And shimmied up the side of a stranger's house until I got close enough to pluck our old cat from edge of the rain gutter.

I held the big fluffy dummy tight against my chest and walked home. Thought, for a fleeting second, about suffocating him. Pushing his purr deep into my belly as I looked up into the clear sky and tried—as always—to count stars, but then I remembered that none of it is up to me. Not cats and their longing to stray. Not big icy winds roaring over Lake Huron. Not anything. And when you know you cannot really do anything to make this place better or worse, it's comforting.

We are bound by nothing.

We may make mistakes, but we can rise above them. We can have bad days, but we can make good ones too. And on days when you aren't feeling particularly thankful, you can always find something that can lift you up. Pull you out of your stupor and make you remember how to forget.

Like the tree out back.

Wet and black.

Swaying in the wind.

Its nine yellow apples hanging on.

To the place where stem meets branch.

Branch meets trunk.

And to the roots buried deep in the ground. Silent and waiting for the last piece of summer to fall.

building a man

Three AM moonlight brightens the world. So much so that our back yard looks as if it's a stage. Dimly lit and waiting. For actors. Characters. For anyone to come out and play. But at three in the morning, I don't feel much like playing. Mostly, I would like to sleep. To be in bed. Temporarily dead. My only sounds some quiet breathing, murmured words, a mumble or two. Like my wife. Warm and gone away from her everyday world that is ruled by kids, a small business, and me.

I am happy she sleeps. Gets recharged and is always fresh. Even. Happy and content.

But standing at the window, feeling the cold reach through the dark pane, does not make me think about being anything. Instead, I wonder if what I'm seeing is true. A small, three-foot-tall snowman is standing by the garage. He is lacking arms. Has no eyes or mouth. Does not have a button nose. But his shape is distinct and he is as real as anything else in the yard.

The orange sled with yellow string.

My boy's red snow shovel.

Dark blots all along the fence line where the dogs run, which can only be one thing.

And amidst all the thoughts that keep me thinking and keep me up at night—bills, my career, fixing things, not writing words that sell—I can't believe I missed the birth of this snowman. He has been built by little hands. Carved out of a bank of snow. Chiseled, sanded, and made into a man by my boy playing all alone.

It is not a good feeling to imagine him out there. Working so hard. Making this man to show the world and having nobody recognize his work. Not even his Dad.

I walk a path from the house to the garage at least four times a day. To haul armloads of wood. To turn on and off Christmas lights. To take out the trash. To get tools. And yet, in the past three days—the last time I remember the snow just being snow—I have not noticed what my boy has done. His building of this man.

It is a brutal reality that punches me hard as I stand in the kitchen. Center of the breakfast nook. Looking out that big dark window onto the moonlit yard.

My kids, they need so much, and they deserve all of it, and yet I miss moments every day. Things they say. Do. How they feel. And although I know my boy is a big boy and he moves on and on, and every day is a rollercoaster of ups and downs and anticipation and disappointment, I need to do better. Listen more. Watch him closely. Try to understand and remember what it was like. Being a little boy. Feeling alone. Trying to build a man with just your hands and the cold of the world.

People get hurt. Especially when fights are worth fighting. With fists or words. And broken relationships are the casualty of self preservation. And preserving the self is what's important to the whole because one is part of everything. A link in the chain. A seat at the dinner table. The account number through which the money comes and goes. I am not one important thing, but many little unimportant things, and I'm learning as I go. I have always known that I am a drop in the bucket. A snowflake in a winter storm. That I am not special or unique. And that what I'm doing has been done and done and done before.

And out of all the things I've done that could have been done better, I would not change a thing. The past has passed. I haven't got time to go back. And I would not change decisions made because from the dark has come good. I am married to more than words and my kids are not stories. I do not shoot from the hip and I do not throw or take any unnecessary punches. I aim more truly and shoot straighter than ever before. My senses are heightened. And as a father and husband, my capacity for bullshit is at an all-time low.

My road may not be as long and as varied as the roads of other men, but I've travelled enough to know where to find the fish, how to trail deer, and to do what's necessary to avoid sinkholes, skunks, and bears. I know how to take care and how to survive. And when my immediate troops and I approach an uneasy or dangerous situation, I know when to turn back and I know when to sack up and give it a try.

Lately, there has been little turning back. Time is precious. There is only this moment. I know my truth because it is not my own. It is made up of what's good for the good of all. And it starts at home. The daily life. My wife. Our boy and our girl. And right now, that's all that matters. Taking care of our own, so that one day the good spreads and none of us are alone.

I have been alone plenty in my life and most of the loneliest times were when I was surrounded by people I thought I knew. And so, I spent hours and hours every day writing and thinking and figuring through things, hoping one day to make sense of it all. I don't write as much anymore. I don't make the time. Don't need it as much.

And long ago, I realized that trying to make sense of everything only kills a man. And so, what's better and what's best is that I *get it*. I see where it's going. And although I don't know much of anything, I do know that I'm not alone.

If we are truly focused on putting good into this world, we will sometimes create hurt and pain. But we cannot beat ourselves up about it. We must buck up and move on. Some will fall and frustrate. Hold on to the past. The rest of us will rise and understand. That this is our moment. Our one true love.

Big cold coming up and through. Around. Pushing into the warm places. Making us shiver. Shake. Snap to life and wake. So we realize that the weight we carry is real and that no matter what we do, the day-after-day struggle to make ends meet, take care of our kids, and keep the fire going, will be overcome by gravity.

There comes a time like this—37 years deep into a Northern Michigan January—when you recognize the brutality. All those things you wrote about when you were young and tough and fighting and fucking without consequence meant more than you could ever know. Babies die. Wives leave. There is always guilt. And more often than not, there are no apologies. You must take your knocks in silence. Keep your word. And keep your wounds secret. You must get up every morning—sober and sad or happy and hung over—and you must be strong. Directed. Helpful and giving. You must be whatever it is they want you to be. That's what you get paid for. That's what you get laid for. And that's what is written and spoken and known throughout the world. A man must not be afraid of anything.

Not being broken.

Dying young.

Or being alone.

A man must be able to see beyond the moment—10:50 pm, second glass of wine, body revving with fight—and he must be able to remember.

His pretty wife just now entering sleep. His two kids tucked away in dreams. And that he has been given a great gift. To be here now. Pounding the black keys, drinking himself to inspiration, because he wants to be better. For himself. For the art. But mostly, for them.

He is not sure what they will do with all of this—the pages and pages and pages—and it doesn't matter because finally, after all these rejection-letter years, he's got an audience. People who care. Who will be curious. Who'll need to know.

Family. Marriage. Love. These are hard things. They are not boiled down to wins and losses. They are not short-lived, passing things.

Not if you're doing it right.

And doing something right—always—is about doing it for someone else.

There is big cold tonight. It is coming up and through. Around. Pushing into the warm places. Making me shiver. Shake. Snap to life and wake. And the only thing I can do is stay up late. Keep putting logs on the fire. Pace the floors. Check on the kids over and over again. Feel their cheeks and backs to make sure they are warm and breathing. And stand in the dark bedroom listening to my wife. Her deep dreamy breath. As she seeks a better place. One that cannot be overcome by gravity.

Hard to start anywhere when I haven't started in so long. Things—they confuse me. Nearly everything does these days. It is simpler and deeper than all the shit we strive for, yet we reach and reach and reach for more.

I tell myself it's for the kids. My wife. For what it takes to make ends meet, but I'm not so sure anymore.

I never wanted any of this. All I've ever wanted was to write. And writing, for those that don't know anything about it, is much more than writing. It is a way of life. A Code. A letter-to-letter book of verse built on the belief that—no matter what—we keep our troops safe and we keep at the keeping on.

It is not for coffee house hacks wearing black clothes and tapping on laptops.

It is not about self-important pricks reciting verse in small clubs.

It's about wringing the every day through your gut and breaking it down so that you are able to recognize and understand the fundamentals. The base. Using the bits and pieces to push toward and create a better place. If you are not aware, and if you are not a fighter committed to digesting the space between night and day, I suspect you will not get it.

I stopped my four-year-old son in the doorway. Between kitchen and dining room. Knelt down. Grabbed him by the shoulders and looked him in the eye.

"Julian, I love you."

He squirmed a little. Smiled.

"No, listen, buddy. Really. I love you."

He relaxed. Cocked his head to one side. Smiled.

"Really? You do?" he asked.

And I felt bad. Like a shit. What kid, I thought, disbelieves the love of his Dad?

"Yes, I love you! You're my boy. I'm here for you always. I've got your back."

I pulled him close. Hugged him tight. Tried to kiss him on the cheek.

"Don't kiss me!" he said.

He smiled. Laughed. Squirmed and pushed himself away from me. And ran.

"I don't love *you*!" he shouted.

He did not mean it. Could not have known or understood the weight of words he said.

And yet, it has made its way to here—this place. My one and only solace. Nine minutes to eleven. Two glasses into the night.

"If your kids don't hate you once in awhile, you're doing something wrong."

That's what my father-in-law said to me. About two o' clock on a Sunday afternoon.

We were sitting in a bar, drinking and eating, watching the Lions do their absolute best to lose another game.

"That makes sense," I said.

"You can't let it get you down," he said.

"I know. I try not to."

"Listen, K.J., it takes work and patience and a whole lot of shit that you can't know until you're in it."

I polished off my vodka tonic. Ordered another. Calvin Johnson dropped a pass.

"It takes more than I ever thought it would," I said.

We said nothing for a long time because men, when they are together—truly together—often do not need words. We communicate silently. Like boxers fighting shadows. Coyotes chasing their tails.

"It will only get better," he said. "The love grows more and more each day. And sometimes, it will hurt because they will not love you back."

It sounded strange to me—kids not loving their parents—because I was sure that all through my life, no matter what, I had loved mine.

But that's what you tell yourself when you're wearing the parent shoes. When you're 37 years old. Married. Have two kids. And would give anything for them.

Your life.

Your dreams.

That small thing that gives you so much hope.

It is so hard to start because I haven't started in so long. These things—the daily moments—they confuse me so much. But I hold fast and I know—deep in that place between night and day—that it is simpler and deeper than all of this. That the shit we strive for but cannot reach means nothing because all we have ever needed and wanted and hoped for was love.

And I had it tonight.

In the doorway.

Between kitchen and dining room.

My boy. Four years old. Not loving me.

Closed on the house. Finally, it is ours. The work is not done, of course. It never is. There will be updates. Improvements. The house, over time, will become part of us and we will become part of it. And so now, we begin the lifelong task of putting down roots. Taking care. Doing whatever we can to keep ourselves upright, thriving and safe, so that we can keep at this keeping on.

This is a good house. For writing. For art. For raising kids. And it will be interesting to see how our lives unfold. The little feet running along hardwood floors today will soon be grown and running out the door. We will experience great loss and great happiness. Day-after-day, this place will be filled with breaths and heartbeats. Laughter and desire. There will good days. There will be bad. But no matter what, we will be together. Pushing ahead. Me and S.B., Little Man and Oogie.

But all of that is too far off for serious thought. When a man gets too caught up in tomorrow, he forgets today. The moment. And right now, the moment has me here. At this. Fingers to the keys. Thoughts churning. Cylinders warming and getting ready to run strong throughout the day. Since five AM, we've been at it. Scrawling pen against paper. Trying to get things straight and reset from another week spent in a cube. And this—a window rattling, ice cold morning all alone in the den—is exactly what we need to find the spark that will set the fire in my gut and get me ready for the day. For soon, they will be up—my wife and kids—and there will be nothing that this old house and I can do, but shake away the tireds and go along for the ride.

It is a fine ride—the family life—but it is not for the weak. And I can see how so many fail. How it can get to the point where it no longer works. Where the nights and days share the same cold. When you no longer notice the little feet. And how the world can close in and a man can forget that he is responsible. For everything.

It is hard to keep working and trying and fighting when all you ever really want to do is rest. But these days, there is no time. Life is one big day with no beginning. With no end. Even the time spent asleep does not seem to break the cycle. I cannot see or hear the ticking hands. There is no alarm. No kiss goodnight. No sunshine. No stars twinkling and bright. All of it just keeps going and going.

Once in a while, I find a moment and stop. But these moments are rare and short-lived, and when I finally buck up and make time, I'm not sure what it's for. And so, I write. Pen to paper. Pounding on plastic. And the pages get socked away in a cabinet where they grow in number each day.

"Why do you keep printing all of this stuff?" S.B. once said to me.

"I don't know," I said. "I just do."

There was a time in my life when I believed I'd make a living at this. Book signings. Readings. My stories winning awards, making lists. But that was long ago when I thought my writing was for everybody. That it would be strong enough and have enough meaning that it would carry me, my friends, and my family to places we'd otherwise never know.

Pretty idealistic. And selfish too.

It's funny how things change when you get a little older. More comfortable in your skin. When all that really matters is that you're alive, making ends meet, and that your wife and kids are smiling more days than not. It is not perfect. Not any of this. And to spend your life planning and hoping and figuring gets you nowhere but farther from the place you've always wanted to be.

Home. Setting down deep roots. So that finally, you can say, *it is ours*. Of course, the work is not done. It never is. There will be updates. Improvements. Over time, you will become part of it and it will become part of you. But right now, all you have to do is take care. Do what it takes. To keep yourself upright. Your wife and kids safe and thriving. So that all of you are happy despite the work not done.

the company we keep

The big orange sun burst and glowed as it pushed up over Lake Huron. I stood there—at the dining room window—scratching my belly, watching it, and tried to remember the last time I watched the sun rise or set. It is such a simple, important thing. And yet, day after day, I miss it.

The orange did not last long. The heavy gray sky has pushed it away. There is a bit of soft pink above rooftops on First Avenue, but it is fading and it will be gone. And we will begin another cold, snowy day in Michigan.

It may be the last hold of winter. It could be the daily grind. It might be that I have too much work to do that is not mine. Whatever it is, it has its grip on me and has me feeling the pinch of time.

But a man cannot wake feeling this way. He must push it aside. Bury it. Buck up. Bite his tongue. And take pride in swallowing his pride.

It is Saturday morning. My boy is munching and slurping cereal. Rattling his spoon around the inside of his bowl as if he's playing the drums. Seriously, in love with his food.

"Mmmmmm … oh, mmmmmm," he says.

My wife just came in, looking pretty and fresh, and feeling good to touch.

"How long have you been up?" she said.

We hugged. Kissed.

"Since four, I guess."

And the little one, she is just waking. Humming and talking. Stretching and rolling around in her crib. Ready to put feet to the floor and shake the earth.

☼

Me—in bed this morning. Awake for hours. The small dog in the basement barking. A modest WOOF every few seconds. And the female cat howling. Their noise a perfect accompaniment to my brain spinning round and round.

I gotta lose weight.

I should start running.

WOOF.

MEEEEROOOOW!

I need to finish editing DC's book.

I have a dozen quotes to finish for work.

WOOF.

MEEEEROOOOW!

I have to replace the light switches in the mud room.

I have to help S.B. get that old tile up and out of the bathroom.

WOOF.

MEEEEROOOOW!

I gotta focus on Real Estate Principles & Practices so I can take the test.

When am I going to ever get back to writing again and when will I publish?

WOOF.

MEEEEROOOOW!

And so, downstairs I went. To let out the barking dog. Tell the horny cat to shut up. And to think of how strange it is that I sleep so little, am awake so much, but never get anything done.

Four turned into five and turned into six and turned into seven and all of it always turns into this. A few moments alone. To pound on the keys. Drink coffee in peace. To think about all the things that need to be done. And position myself so I remember that in the whole scheme of things, most of it doesn't matter anyway.

What matters are the things you never forget.

Like seeing the sun rise. Over water, the rooftops, the trees.

Your son loving cereal so much.

Your wife's kiss and hug.

Your little daughter's heavy feet.

And feeling the hope and perspective that all of it brings. Because these days—no matter how good or bad they may be—do not last. And sooner than later, the sights and sounds that make up the memories of our lives will be gone. Pushed away into the fading pink of the morning sky.

There is so much life before we die.

And even the gray has gone now. The world is white with big fluffy flakes. They are falling. Down and down and down. Winter keeps piling up. The kids are watching cartoons. My wife is brushing her teeth. The dog is at my feet. And all we can do is wait it out. Do good work and enjoy the company we keep.

My boy has a loose tooth. My daughter refuses to use the potty. My wife is so pretty it hurts. And still, hours after work has ended, I am wrapped up in it. Thinking on quotes and phone calls. Emails and orders. Aware of the startling fact that because I've become so consumed by it, it is now consuming me.

I woke this morning after four hours of sleep. Showered. Dressed. Brushed my teeth. But soap and water, fresh clean clothes and fluoride could not wash away the numbers, the deadlines, the heavyweight punch that had somehow socked me and left me feeling beat down. Dead tired. Whooped.

And so, I stayed home from work only to work more than I work when I'm at work. The day was a rush. A blur. A flurry of conversation and keystrokes, and at quarter after five, S.B., my sweet, came into the den.

"Honey, are you going to stop?"

"I'm done," I said. "I'm just listing priorities for tomorrow."

I felt like a shit saying it. Knew that I should have quit already. But when you are driven to please, you will do stupid, silly things. Like hole yourself up in a cube, in an office, your very own home, so that you can earn a paycheck, get a bonus, and believe that you are only doing what's necessary and right, and that you are not alone.

"You started earlier than usual," she said. "You worked through lunch. It's after five and the kids and I are hungry."

She rubbed my shoulders. Touched my neck. Brought me back and down to the simple, real, meaningful Earth.

Time. Family. Hunger.

And I wonder why I wonder when it is something I already know.

A candle cannot burn at both ends for long. There are only so many hours in the day. Wax does not last. And sooner or later, all flames go out. And when time is up and you are left sitting there, alone in the dark, what will you remember?

The quote that went late? The deal you did not close? The list of phony priorities that keeps waking you night after night so that you feel the great weight of the world crushing you?

Or will you remember …

Your boy's loose tooth.

Your daughter's small victories on the potty.

And how lucky you are to be spending your days with a woman so beautiful it hurts.

<u>*one key at a time*</u>

Nicholas Sparks writes 2000 words a day. Five or six days a week. It takes him three to eight hours to do this. He is rich. Famous. And I suppose I should add, he's a good writer. Our friend, Nick, also reads at least 100 books a year.

He is a machine.

He must not sleep.

He has somehow got a leg up on time.

I got up earlier than the rest of the tribe this morning. Had to. I owe Mr. Coyote a final version of his edited book. Have two other books that need editing—a children's book and a novel. And I wanted to do this—bang away at the keys, put things into perspective, and make myself believe that one day, I'll be a writer too.

Not today, but one day.

There are the projects that belong to others that I need to complete. There is a house that needs my hands for remodeling. There is Little Man and Oogie that need constant attention. And there is S.B., my wife. The woman that brings it all together. The straw that stirs the drink. And she needs time for her art, her business, her sanity.

In short, there is not enough time in the day. We are all loving and growing and building and being happy, but also we are all headed to that place where light and dark meet and we leave for good. And so, we must pick and choose our battles. Focus—but not too much—on what it is we want to do. What makes us happy. And for me this morning, it is *this*. Being here. Drinking coffee. Watching snowflakes whirl around.

The flakes are as dazed and confused as the doves on the roof of the house next door. Yesterday, it was rain and 40s. Today we have snow and below freezing. It is too cold for mating or flying, for pecking around on the ground, and so the puffed-up doves sit under the eaves cooing questions back and forth. The flakes loop and swirl, fall and stick, and one-by-one they are growing.

Things change fast around here. Ours is a focus aimed on the moment. There is not a clear picture of the future. And so, we pound away at the small tasks at hand. Toys growing out of the floor. Stains on the furniture. Snotty noses. Tender gums. The humorous defiance of a five-year old as he stakes his claim to the world. And the monumental test of patience required for a 21-month old girl that believes the world stops when she throws a tantrum.

But we all feel like that sometimes.

Like putting on our new Star Wars boxers and superhero t-shirt, shoving our little sister out of the way and throwing pillows and toys and jumping up and down on the couch and shouting, *"I'm the boss! I'm ruler of the universe! I am Star Wars and Incredible Hulk and nobody can stop me!"*

And we feel like this too.

Like falling to the ground. Crying. Staying there. Reveling in the smell of high-traffic carpet. Wishing that everybody would just leave you alone, but also that everybody would come on over and pick you up too. That you could somehow stay there in your moment of sadness, all eyes upon you, and have the sympathy of the world. That life would stop and wait and be there with big hugs when you're ready to get up and get moving again.

But everything is moving. There isn't anything that ever really stops. And although our movements are subtle and small in this ebb and flow, this round and round, we keep pushing along.

Some of us are Nicholas Sparks with our 2000 words a day and our 100 books a year. Others, like me, have this—half an hour before the family wakes and the day begins. Almost seven hundred words of another day of moment-after-moment perspective. Not rich. Not famous. Not anything at all. Just another man keeping at the keeping on, banging away at life—one key at a time—before light comes to meet the dark for good.

all of us together

Damp and gray and still. It could be a November afternoon or an April morning. But the grass is greening. Buds and flowers rising. And the birds are coming around. In number and song and on these mornings—rain, snow, or shine—I can hear them and see them. Robins, starlings, sparrows. Jockeying for position, squabbling, singing, and soaring. Gathering sticks and string, paper and leaves for nests. Chasing each other for fun, for fight, for no reason at all, but for the simple fact that they are faster and freer and more capable than most. And when the trees and sky and earth are your home, and you can move over it and above it with ease, the dangers become minimal and there is beauty and peace.

There has to be.

Flight, feathers, and hollow bones cannot only be a matter of survival. There's more to it than that. And maybe birds, with their small brains in the wide-open world, understand it better than us—the big-brained mammals. And maybe we should look to the sky and observe more often. Or simpler yet, maybe we ought to stop and just think awhile.

Not about us, but about them—the people and creatures that spend their lives with us day after day.

In short, it's about being nice, as childish as that seems. It's about listening and hearing and recognizing that our actions, reactions, and inactions have a profound effect on the world. What you put out there—what you say and do—lasts. It may be forgotten, but it will last and it will create a change that cannot be undone. And the only redemption we have is to admit our mistakes—at least to ourselves—and then move ahead with honest, honorable intent, so that we do not make the same mistakes again. We must tell ourselves, pledge to ourselves, that we will do better. But people, as far as I can tell, are creatures of habit. Lazy in thought. Weak in the gut. And most don't have the ability to recognize the most subtle things, the little things. And when people are unable to sit and think awhile of things outside themselves—the way the sky changes throughout the day, how still a tree can be, the great strength of feathers and hollow bones—then it's unlikely they will ever break their patterns, see the need to change, and make the choices that we, as big-brained mammals, need.

Every day, we are faced with choices. Put in situations. Given the great gift of opportunity. The chance to interact with family, friends, co-workers, and strangers. And every day, because of our mood, our feelings, our desires, we dismiss opportunities to communicate, to learn, to live a life outside ourselves with others.

One of the worse things a person can do is go through life feeling that they are the center. That they are in charge, the focus, the deserving one. That somehow—because of who they believe they are—they deserve something better. And, although it is important to listen and hear these people, and it is important to play nice in this world, sometimes the only thing you can do to help someone is knock them down. With fist. With words. With an accident or great tragedy. Sometimes, you can do it on your own—drag a belligerent misogynist out of a bar and clock him. Other times, you can do it with words—succinctly and honestly, so they cut, not like a dagger, but like a surgeon's tool. And other times, it takes Mother Nature or God. And even when these two have to get involved, it may not be enough. And if you will not let yourself be broken—if you cannot learn to love—then you run the great risk of being broken for good.

And there is no coming back from that.

White light pushes away the damp and gray. The sun rises over Lake Huron. There is hope and possibility today. I can hear it and see it. In numbers, words, and song. All of us together. Jockeying for position. Gathering together the bits and pieces of whatever it takes to make our home. Chasing each other for fun, for fight, for no reason at all, but for the simple fact that we are faster and freer and more capable than most. And when the trees and sky and earth are your home, and you can move over it and above it with ease, the dangers become minimal, and there is beauty and peace.

There has to be.

to remember, believe, and come back to

It's about luck. And technique. Having a voice that strikes deep. And it is about nothing at all. Men have made more money doing easier things. Women have loved more famous men. And trying to think about this—any of it—three glasses into the night, is senseless.

There is only so much we can do.

Especially when nobody expects anything. And when those that do expect things expect them for themselves, not you.

Tonight, there is darkness and rain, and my fingers are hungry.

Where are you?

I want to feel the icy cold of Lake Huron. To plunge and sink and wait for light to break the surface and pull me up from the bottom so that I can see again how special it is to breathe and hear and walk through Kmart on a Thursday night with Little Man, Oogie, and S.B. The kids jacked up and unruly, and my wife all curls, green eyes, and smiling.

Sand for the sandbox.

Oil filter for the car.

Sheets, pillow cases, and a comforter for Oogie because she is ready to make the move from baby crib to big girl bed. And I want to get something for Little Man, but he has made his transition from baby to boy and already has a bed full of SpongeBob and Spider-Man. And besides, I've made him a deal—that we will go fishing this weekend if he can be good and respectful, and if he can love and protect Momma and Oogie while I'm gone to work each day.

And it will work no matter what because all a Dad ever wants to do is go fishing with his son. No matter if the he's been bad or good. So, we will sit near the river. Stand on the lakeshore. We will cast. Drown bait. And we will have something.

To remember.

Believe.

Come back to.

Like when a man is pushing 40, getting better at picking his battles, putting everyone first, but still clinging to unreachable things. Hopes and dreams. Big ones that are supposed to make him rich and famous, even though the richest he's ever been was when simple moments grabbed hold.

Fishing with Dad.

Falling asleep to the smell of fresh sheets.

Drinking wine with old friends.

And living smack dab in the middle of the American Dream. A place he swore he would never be.

But here I am.

In love. Being loved.

Lucky with technique. Striking deep. And realizing that all of this nothingness is everything. And everything is all we can do.

pure joy

It should be handwritten. Inked to paper. Set aside. Left for them to read if they ever choose to read and learn—to know how it used to be—but it has been a long time, another great distance, and when mood and moment synch there is often no other way than this.

Trying key after key.

Hunting and pecking until the letters meet, relate, make some sense, and push us.

On.

To unlock.

The next moment. So we are clean and clear. Interested in this time.

The now.

Our small existence. In this small town. Where we live a life so simple and rich—so free and connected to the earth—that there is nothing about it that can be believed.

My kids are healthy. Happy. And they make me see that I am important. Somebody. I am the strongest. The smartest. The fastest. And there is nobody that can hug or help or love like me. Except Mommy. And she, I'll admit, is better than me.

At patience.

Consistency.

Softness.

Beauty.

The artful act of pure joy.

And because she has given them to me—our boy and our girl—it seems there is nothing I'll ever be able to do to make her know how much she means to me.

I cannot birth babies.

Paint pictures.

Make sushi.

Mediate.

Keep the faith.

Bring as much good to the world as she does.

And still, she loves me.

To know this—to experience it—is amazing.

I have come a long way in a short while. I am lucky to be alive. The fists, the fights, the self-imposed, self-destructive nights after nights after nights have somehow landed me here. Home. Deep into the place I never knew could be.

So worthy of words.

Handwritten. Inked to paper. And set aside. For when my endurance has run out and I am only stacks of pages left for you to read. Letter strung to letter. Key meeting key. So that you will know how it used to be.

one bad day

He's lost it a little. That something that pushed and pushed and pushed him. It was light. But there was deep darkness too. Days did not end or begin. They only moved seamlessly one into another. And now that he is full and filling out—heavier, slower, more patient with the world—he has so much of what he needs that wanting—feeling the urge to fight, fuck, and be free—seems selfish. Silly.

Desire, he believes, is something for youth. And his youth is fading. Things are not as tight. Steady. As dependable and strong. He does not get and cannot take what he wants because his job is to be giving. To do whatever it takes for his family to be happy, healthy, and safe. And though he finds great satisfaction in giving them a better life than he had as a kid—a better life than he, himself, now deserves—he wonders sometimes if he'll ever get it back. If he's lost it at all.

Maybe it's in the river.

He thought this tonight as he and his wife spent the one hour they had without kids walking around the old town that he has loved and hated for so long.

"You want to stop in at The Lau for a drink," she asked.

"No," he said, and looked up at the sky that was moving quickly from light to dark. "We only have half an hour left, and you say you never get to walk the North Side."

"Are you sure?"

He wasn't. Never is. What is there to be sure about in this life, except for love?

For your wife.

Your kids.

Your family.

A few friends.

"I'm sure," he said.

And so, instead of drinking, they walked. And walked. Past the Lau, St. Mary's, and up Miller Street. Past shitty old houses. The dead bakery. And around the skate park, where kids—just fucking kids—sat, stood, skated, rode bikes, and smoked cigarettes. He wanted to walk over and slap each and every one of them. Knock sense in and smoke out. But there was no slapping, no fighting, no anything. He and his wife crossed the Ninth Avenue Bridge, and for a moment he thought of Aden and Jake. His two friends from the only decent story he ever wrote. The boys he had made so much like and so much unlike himself that he considered them his own blood.

Until he had kids.

And as he and his wife crossed over the dark water and he thought of what it was like to lose Jake—just a character that he conceived in ratty old booth in Saint Paul, Minnesota—he could not bear the thought of ever losing Oogie. Little Man. S.B. The three of them the only reason he gets up every day, puts one foot in front of the other, and does what's necessary to keep a good, solid roof over their heads. And as he peered down into the swirling depths, he began to feel better.

It has only been a bad day, he thought. One bad one in a string of good ones. It is true that I don't have the time I used to have. That I am not the man I had believed I would be, but even my bad days are good. And time, as evident as it appears in the passing from day to night, is seamless. There is hope. A possibility.

He may have lost a little, but he has a lot. He is full and patient. And he is still learning how important it is to not worry about what he wants, but to be thankful for what he can give.

And tonight, here it is. All of it. Wrapped up in words.

mindful of my roots

You are always thankful. And mindful of your roots. You recognize the great pains of the world, but also know that it is important to laugh. To be considerate. Kind. And yet, there are days—mornings like this—when you really don't give a shit. All you want, all you've ever really wanted was to write and be left alone. And although this desire—like all of your desires—have been tempered by age, marriage, fatherhood, you still want to write. To put words to paper. As useless, as futile, as self-centered as it seems, it is what you are meant to be. And the bitch of it is simply trying to find the time to do it. It is no longer about being successful and making a living doing it. It is not about being published. It's simply about having the goddamned time to write—to do something you love.

Writers do not have cheerleaders. There is no push from your family and friends. They, in the whole scheme of things, do not care if you write or not. They say they just want you to be happy, but what they don't realize is that writing is not about happiness. Writing—mine, anyway—is about all of those things that lead to happiness. I'll not bring you flowers and candy. There'll be no balloons or parades. There will not be slick, formulaic thrillers, or heart fluttering romances. Those things do not last. And as integral as they are to our existence in the form of entertainment, escape, our culture, they are not the guts and bones of life.

And so, I write about the little things. And the little thing today is that it is another sun-drenched, blue-sky Northern Michigan summer day. There is a book to finish. Stories to complete. And there is a girl in a black garbage bag at the bottom of the creek. A father and son are about to find her. They have lost much. A wife. A mother. An unlikely inspiration. They are two men—old and new—struggling to find a way in a world that does not care about loss and does not wait. And nothing—not bears eating drunken men, not half-naked girls, and not even the beaver's instinct to build a dam—can save them. And I'm not sure that the story—*Man's Struggle*—and the rest of the book is enough to save me.

But it is too sunny to think about it now. And there is no alone time in this house—not in any house filled with love and kids and dogs and cats and work and bills and a husband and wife that never get a chance to settle or think or lift their dreams up into the light. And this will likely be it. For today. For a week. For as long as it takes for me to remind myself to be thankful. Mindful of my roots. And be able recognize the great pains of the world without forgetting how important it is to laugh. To be considerate. Kind. And that there will be days—mornings like this—when I really don't give a shit, but I have to. Because my desires—all of my desires—have been tempered by age, marriage, fatherhood. And writing, as important it is to me, is not as important to everyone else. And I must push ahead, steady go, at doing what it takes to keep us afloat. Upright. Safe. And strong.

primed

It comes in big moments. Sixty-mile-an-hour wind gusts. Hail. Lightning blasting the dark sky.

And it comes in little moments as well.

The quiet clicks of small keys beneath my fingers as I work away at more shit that doesn't matter.

The sounds of my boy and my girl. Their voices. Their play. The things that _do_ matter. My solid reminders that life is a great gift, but also the one-two combination that socks me in the gut and makes me fight for breath as time is wrung out, pushed away, and I am left alone knowing that there is not one fucking thing I can do to stop it. Pause it. Save it.

And so, another rainy day passes and I am digging for a new low, heading straight along to the dark of the bottom. A place I am familiar with. Unafraid of. And fond of, because it is one of the best places for a writer to be. Especially when he is tired. Beat. And feeling the urge to create his own truth, his own value, his own appreciation because in the real world these things are hard to see. Life is good. Easy. Everything I never expected it to be. But happiness is the key to a lack of productivity. And the best writers I know work alone and from the dark and are able to separate muscle from bone without spilling an ounce of blood. And so, it is time to push even harder to see what it is we can break without causing irreparable harm. There is not enough wine, enough lack of sleep, enough of anything to kill me, so I should be able to cruise along fast and hard until the end of December. By the end of the year, I should have the new short story book completed. And what, exactly, does that mean? Nothing. Just because it will be finished does not mean that it will be published. And because it may not be published it will likely go unread. But still, I will have done something for me. And sometimes the best things a man can do are for himself. Things that nobody understands, agrees with, or can believe.

A girl I once knew told me that I think too much. That I put too much effort into caring about things that don't matter.

"We work to pay bills and make ends meet," she said. "That's it. You take life too serious. You're thinking and writing about things that you can't change and you're missing out on having fun. Your dream of being a writer is eating you alive."

"You're a fucking dummy," I said.

She stood there. Mouth open. Eyes watering up. Coffee mug shaking in her hand. This was a big shock to her because the night before she had told me she loved me.

"I am not."

"Yes, you're a dummy. You don't get it. And if you could put any thought into the world outside of your fingernails, belongings, and your hair, then maybe what you just told me would make me give a shit."

"I can't believe you're saying this to me."

"Well, believe it. I'm sick and tired of people telling me that I take life too serious and that I'm missing out on things when all everyone seems to do is plug through this fucking world tied down to things that make them unhappy."

"Do I make you unhappy?"

She was trembling now. Sad, but also very, very angry.

"No. You don't make me unhappy, but I cannot find any happiness in what we have."

"And what is it that you think we have?" she asked.

"We haven't got anything," I said.

The coffee mug smashed against the floor. She turned. Walked away. And I never saw her again. I had been on a week-long drinking and writing bender. Had slept very little. But had just finished the last in a string of short stories that would be published as *Infidelity* and got myself neck deep in the stories that would become *Pilgrim's Bay*. I had been to work every day at my real job from three to 11. At the bar from 11 to two. Finished breakfast with Lunde or Holt every night by four. And then I wrote until at least noon. I would wake a half hour before work to shit, shower, and shave, and then I would do it all again.

That was ten years ago. Some say my prime. But the people that say this don't know me. Those that *do* know me—and there are very few—understand that what I'm doing is something that cannot be accomplished in five, ten, or fifteen years. What I'm doing takes a lifetime. And it comes in moments so big or so small that there is nothing I can do to prepare for it and so always, I am alert and aware. Watching and listening. For thunder and lightning in the late August sky. And my kids—their voices, their play—just before the storm pushes through. And I am thankful for the things that matter. The solid reminders that life is a great gift but it is also full of one-two combinations that sock you in the gut and make you fight for breath as time is wrung out, pushed away, and you are left knowing that there is not one thing you can do to stop it. Pause it. Save it from happening.

If you wait, you miss out.

On the big orange sun pushing up over 100-year old rooftops and the sleeping trees. First thing in the morning, as you make the same five-block walk you do every day, Monday through Friday. Thankful to be alive. Happy to be able to make ends meet. Maybe a little too content, because you're gaining weight and showing gray and you are accepting more downs and outs and accidents and shit than you ever have before.

This.

All of this. The great move from being alone to being loved. An act that is still new and heavy and more intimate and real than anything you have ever known. But an act that feels tried and true, worn with comfort, as if it's the thing you've always done in the place you've always been meant to be.

And life, the older I get, is more happy than sad. More awake than asleep. More promising and hopeful than the life I had when I was younger, had aim, but no intent.

I am meant for great things

Just ask my kids. My son, at night. After I give him his good night hug.

"Boy time tomorrow!" he says.

"Yes, we'll have boy time," I say. "I love you. Good night. See you tomorrow."

"Love you, too. See you tomorrow," he says. "And don't forget boy time!"

"I won't," I say. And I shut his door.

And I think of how good it is to have someone want nothing more than to be with me. My son and I can play Batman, Go Fish, draw pictures, play catch, or just sit side-by-side on the couch flipping channels doing nothing. And he loves me. It is something I take seriously. That I do not take for granted. And that feeds me.

Like my daughter tonight. Sitting by my side at B & B BBQ. Eating mac n' cheese, smoked brisket, seasoned fries, and pickles—everything I had on my plate—and smiling.

"You like Daddy's food?" I asked, as I wiped her mouth with my napkin.

"Uh-huh," she said. Nodded. Smiled. Her blue eyes striking deep. Making me remember how lucky any of us are to just be here.

On this earth.

Plugging away.

Waking and working. Breathing. Surviving. Making ends meet. Walking to work. Earning a living. Then coming home. Hugging your wife. Smelling her. Feeling her curls against your cheek, your neck, your soul. Kissing her. Hugging your son. Reveling in his smile. Then seeing your little girl, two years old and happy, walking past you, through the kitchen, wearing the shoes that you've just worn all day.

"I go to work now, Daddy," she says.

And it is cute and lasting and means so much that it makes its way into you and out of you, to the keys. The place that feels so familiar. Where everything is shiny and new.

Too much of a few things. Not enough of others. Greens are moving toward browns and reds. Days are shorter. And each morning there appears a little more gray. Pushing through the sky above Lake Huron. Easing into my temples.

Another month is nearly gone. Autumn imminent. Winter threatening. The grand cycle continues and I haven't noticed in a long while because I haven't been living.

"I've been busy," I say.

And I have.

I know it. I feel it in my shoulders, my back, in my feet as I pace away the early hours while everyone else sleeps. The floor feels softer in the dark when I'm barefoot and barely moving. The windows are clearer. The ceiling and walls more comforting. And it's only then, standing in the living room at 3:00 in the morning, when I'm looking out at this quiet, sleepy town, that it hits me.

The stars are so bright.

The sky wide open and waiting.

And our dot on the map is warmed only by a corner streetlight that flickers like a candle.

I am small. Just a man. Nothing.

And this big world will keep on keepin' on without me. It will not wait. And if I ever want anything more for me—for my family— this is it. My only shot to get it right and do all things I dream of. But dreams don't come easy when you're just about 40. When you're married. Have kids. And you work most of your days bridging a gap that has ends that barely meet, never overlap, and leave you thinking and restless deep into the night, so that you find yourself in your boy's room, kneeling down at his bed, watching him sleep. Touching his face. Kissing the top of his head.

Whispering.

"You're a good boy. You'll be fine. I love you."

And then to your daughter's room. To pull covers up to her shoulders. Kiss her cheek. Wonder what it is that a two-year old dreams. And quietly say, "I love you, Oogie. Sweet dreams."

You stand in that long hallway between the door to the rest of the world and the door to the bedroom where the woman you love sleeps soundly in your warm bed. And even though it is only a small town, where every hope, expectation, and opportunity is something you—yourself—must create, grow and own, you cannot wait to get back out there and try again. First though, because you have found this comfort in the darkest part of morning, you must rest. At least for a few hours. So you ease into bed. Put your arm around your wife, and you fall away into sleep believing you are the on the right track. Doing the right things. Being the man they need.

But that's okay. And all of this is part of it. The first 38 years—all those days—have led to this. A gray, still morning in September. With me, up and at it. The way it's supposed to be. Ready to reach deep into my bag of tricks and make something happen. Because life lately, has been too much of a few things. Not enough of others. And a man only gets one chance to notice how hard summer works. To give to us hope. As we move into the colors of Autumn. The season for reaping what we've sown.

dad's birthday

Dad turns 60 today. I wonder what it would be like. To wake that far into it. Knowing that you've lived longer than your father. Longer than other relatives. Friends. I wonder how a man feels on the morning of his 60th birthday. In a quiet warm house on The Ridge. Does he think on the chores that need to be done? On frost that's coming on thicker every day? Does he reflect on the years turned into memories? Or, by the time a man has turned 60, is all of the thinking replaced by simple happiness? The joy of being alive.

This is something I cannot know. Might be something I'll never know. And even if I make it to 60, my days cannot be like my Dad's because we are different men. We share the same blood. The same values. But we have had and do have different lives.

Dad's life was harder.

He had a harder upbringing. Had to work harder for food, clothing, and the roof he kept over our heads. And throughout his life, Dad's made decisions that most men do not have the guts to make. Some of them, I know about, as I grew up watching his every move. And though as a kid I could not understand the implications and complications of those decisions, I understand them now.

Life, being a man, is about making commitments and keeping them. You learn this when you marry. And if you take marriage seriously by having fun and growing and honing the art of compromise, you will stay married a long time. Dad has done this. For 39 years, he has made good on his vows. Made more good decisions than bad. And his dedication and devotion to his wife has brought him more beauty, peace, and good than most men will ever know.

Some will scoff at this. Some will not see this, understand it, believe it, but those are the people that don't know my Dad. And, I'm afraid; those are the same people that don't anything about love because they have never loved anything more than themselves. My Dad knows a thing or two about what it takes. To sacrifice. Endure. Be the man, husband, friend, and silent leader that's required to fight the good fight, keep a family strong, and make the subtle, lasting things that carry on.

He scrawled notes at five in the morning, before work, for his wife and kids to read. Short lists of chores. Congratulations for passing a test or doing something—anything—right. I love yous and funny pictures. Marks on paper that have imprinted themselves into me.

Throwing the football back-and-forth and back-and-forth. Saying nothing. Just a ball, me and my Dad. Playing catch as the big orange sun tucked itself in for another night.

A pat on the back and twenty bucks stuffed in my shirt pocket when I finally came home to visit after being God-knows-where for so long.

Harsh words and hard guidance when needed.

"You're drinking too much. It'll ruin you. Knock it off, dumbshit. Believe me, I know."

And before I know it, all those things Dad has said and done—most of it silently and without me ever knowing—have made it deep into my blood, my gut, my life. And what I've learned from him is that all a man can ever do to make sure that he has no regrets is to put *them* first. And by them—I mean everyone.

Your wife. She comes first. It may not always be easy. More often than not, you will compromise. But your wife is the person that knows you better than anyone. Maybe even better than yourself. Give up the macho bullshit. Be honest. Listen. Learn about her and do what it takes to make sure she is appreciated. Feels loved. And knows that you are there for her. That you are a team. For today, tomorrow, and to the end. You are her rock.

Your kids. You get up in the morning every day and you go to work so that your kids can have all the opportunity, possibility, and hope that you can afford them. Do not miss a moment. The good, the bad—all of it, is good. You will think about them, worry about them, and want the best for them. And until you are gone away into the big deep sleep that consumes all, they will be in your care.

Everyone. We only have this one shot. Some of us have longer than others. And a man must do what it takes, day after day, to be there. For his family. His neighbors. His friends. And as he moves along through the days of his life, what he learns—often by accident and tumultuous battles of trial-and-error—is this:

There are times to step up, to step in, but most importantly, a man must know when to step back. To keep his mouth shut. Listen. Put others first. And to do his best at aiming truly and following through, so that one day, maybe on the morning of his 60th birthday, he will wake happy with a head full of thoughts and a heart full of feelings that nobody else can know and that nobody can ever take away And he can feel good because maybe, just maybe, someone has been listening too.

A wife, a daughter, a son.

And they will be thankful for his hard work. His love. For all he has done.

Like I am.

Dad, you turn 60 today. And I wonder what it will be like. When I wake that far into it. Knowing that I've outlived family. Friends. That things have come and gone. That so much time has passed.

Will I think about the chores that need to be done?

Will I think about the Spring that has come and gone?

Or will I reflect on all the years that have turned into memories and simply be happy to be alive?

I'm not sure. I'm not there yet. But I will get there, Dad. And I will do so by sticking on the path that you have worked so hard to clear on your way to becoming a man.

Happy Birthday, Dad.

thanksgiving day, 2011

I am thankful for frost on rooftops. Unraked leaves. Ten yellow apples hanging on the tree. That's one more than last year on this day. And this is our second Thanksgiving in Alpena. The town we left as young adults, but came back to with our kids so that they would be grounded. Humbled. Always within reach of nature. Because the things you learn in a small town, surrounded by family and friends, are things that last. The lessons are subtle. Often silent. And brutality—because there is less of it—is more profound.

Theft.

Vandalism.

Violence.

Car accidents.

These things are still news. And although we don't have as many conveniences or thrills as other places, what we have seems to work. There could be more investment in the town. More opportunity. More jobs. This town could be bigger, healthier, more in tune with the outside world. But the longer I'm here, the more I realize that this is not what the people want.

Not yet.

Once the old money dies or is passed on to younger hands, things will change because that money will disappear. It will leave town or be consumed by the mouths and desires connected to those hands. It will not be shared. Saved. Doled out over time. And even though I know that the money, investment, and opportunity really doesn't matter, I fear that the desire I have for my kids to be grounded, connected, thoughtful, and resourceful may jeopardize opportunities they may have elsewhere. That my desire to have them firmly rooted in a small town that I loved, hated, and loved again will be a handicap, a roadblock, their eventual undoing. That even though the schools are good, people care, and a strong few are trying to step up and make change for the good, unless we are vigil about aiming our kids away from Alpena, they may never reach their heights.

Is there any good in being a Big Fish in a small pond?

I see Big Fish washing up every day. Frustrated men with ruddy complexions that have hard hands and even harder souls because at one time they were on top of their game. High school big shots.

Athletes. And they were loved and fun and got away with all sorts of things because they were everybody's All-American. Not bad guys, but Big Fish in this little pond, and now they are rotting from the inside out because they drink too much, care too little, and spend their lives working factory jobs, doing construction work, or sliding by on odd job after odd job after odd job, hating everyone else for the life they've made.

A general description. An easy—and some will say—inaccurate insight. But I know more men like this and the women that are affected by them than I do any other kind. This town, even if I'm off a few degrees here and there in words of description, is full of these Big Fish. And now, on Thanksgiving, I am thankful that I'm not one of them. That I never was or will be a Big Fish anywhere. And I am thankful that we came back. Made sacrifices so that our kids could start out on a stable foundation that has been years and years in the making. Because it isn't about conveniences and having more things to do. More buildings and more people do not equal more opportunity. What it's about is starting small and never losing sight of the simple things.

And being thankful.

For frost on rooftops.

Unraked leaves.

Ten yellow apples hanging on the tree.

That's one more than last year.

And this is our second Turkey Day in Alpena. The town that has somehow kept us grounded. Humbled. Always within reach of nature. Surrounded by the things that last.

hope for miles

The big sky is holding out. Heavy and gray two days ago. So low, I could touch it. Then, last night, walking home, it was clear. Blue. Easing to soft pink and orange, as the sun slipped over the edge of the earth, leaving the last signs of hope for the day.

And this morning, I wait.

For the sky to break and move us from this season in between. So there is clarity.

In the fall, I know what to do. It is about preparation. Caulk and plastic sheets. Chainsaw and the ax. Preserving food. Stocking the shelves. Loading the freezer with meat.

But now, we are here. Slugging through these strange days. Preparation complete. The sky a great thing of suspense and intrigue. And it's getting harder to recognize and reach for the simple things. And I wonder sometimes if everything I've been saying for years is shit. That maybe, all of the things we have convinced ourselves to do—work, earn, marry, pay bills, reproduce, pray, create, and love unconditionally—are not for our benefit, but for the well-being of those around us.

But you cannot understand this when you are alone. Doing those things to prepare for a life better lived. When you are not in it. When you are drunk as much as sober. In the dark more than the light. When life is a steady buzz of selfishness, great highs and great lows, and acts of self-destruction bring you just enough of the things you need to be happy, even if only for a little while. Pretty, willing girls. Nights on the town. More drinks—round after round—and recognition for *everything* you do. Pay raises at work. Pats on the back for a job well done. Handshakes and hugs all around for stories published in magazines or books that you knew would never matter. Because all of the things you do when you are egotistical and fighting fights not worth fighting are important and true. And when you are living so freely, but with so much hollow space inside of you, you are able to see those simple, perfect things.

Because you don't have them.

Like I do. Now. In this strange season that I know will not last.

A bumble bee sticker on the door of my writing room. Placed at the height of my two-year old. And all I want to do is hug her. Hold her. Try to imagine what it must be like to be so small and happy and sure.

And my boy last night, as I tucked him in.

"Dad, I have something to ask you," he said.

"Sure, buddy. What's up?"

He smiled. Pulled the covers up to his chin.

"Tomorrow, after you get home from work, can we have some boy time?"

"Yes, we sure can."

And I kissed his cheek. Gave him a hug. And went into the living room feeling pretty goddamned good.

There was the fire, warm and comforting. And there was S.B., so pretty on the couch that it shot lightning through my veins and hurt. And I marveled at the fact that she and I made vows to last and last, and somehow we keep it going, on the right path.

The night went as well as it can for any man. We drank wine. Talked. Watched some senseless television show. Then went to bed, side-by-side. Another day gone, but another one too, waiting just over the horizon.

And here it is. The beginning of another in this in-between season. And I'm waiting for the big sky to give it up. So that there is less of the gray. More oranges. Pinks. The clear blue. So that I can build up the reserves and be thankful for all I've got.

The ability to work and earn.

A solid, growing marriage.

A roof over our heads.

Healthy kids.

And all around me—no matter what I say or do—three people love me most. And it's the unconditional kind that does exactly what it's supposed to.

Keep a man balanced.

And moving.

One foot in front of the other.

From one season to another.

Head up. Heart in the right place.

And nothing but hope for miles.

happy new year

New Year's Day. The party we are at ends early for us. The kids are being kids. First quiet in unfamiliar territory. Then happy and laughing. Some snacks. A light meal. A couple hours pass and they wind up and wind up and then all at once come crashing down. It is a rush, but not a frenzied one, to leave.

We are used to this. It happens. It's the holidays. The shake up in the schedule. The change in diet. It is not their fault. It is not our fault. It is the way it goes when you have little kids. So, you chase them down. Wrestle them into coats. Wrangle them into boots. Shove hats onto heads. Push hands into mittens. Give hugs. Say quick good-byes. And finally, you are out the door. Carrying them to the car through sleet and snow. The wet cold finding the back of your neck, your fingers, your nose. And after you buckle them in and you and your wife are in the car, you sit—for just a moment—and breathe.

"Love you, honey," I say to S.B.

"Love you too," she says. "Sorry we left before the game was over."

The kids scream. Cry. Bellow about not wanting and wanting to go home.

"It's okay. I think it's on the radio."

S.B. scans SPORTS and lands perfectly on the game. The Lions are driving down the field. There is a chance that they will finally beat Green Bay.

The kids scream. Wail. Bellow some more.

I crank up the defrost. Put the SUV into drive and begin up the long, winding, icy driveway. Little Man, our oldest, the five-year-old, is especially loud. He is pounding his fists and kicking the seat.

"If you don't knock it off, I'm going to stop the car, get out, and come back there."

All this, and we have not even made it out of the drive.

He screams. Pounds. Kicks.

I stop the car. Open my door. Feel the cold rush of January. And walk around to the back of the car. When I open the door, he stops. I put my hand on his shoulder. Look him in the eye.

"Are we done here?"

He smiles.

"Yes, I'm sorry!"

I slam the door. Walk back to my door and get in.

The Lions are still driving. Pushing their way to the goal line.

S.B. pats my hand.

"Sorry," I said. "I shouldn't yell like that. I just wanna get home."

"Drive careful," she says, as I ease up to Nicholson Hill Road and turn left toward US 23.

"It was a good party," I say.

She smiles, "It was. I enjoyed myself."

"And you guys had fun, right?"

"YEA!" they shout. Already, they are heading back up to a high.

"Who likes parties?" I shout.

"MEEEEEE!" we all yell.

That's how it goes with kids. With marriage. With family. Ups. Downs. Crazy uneven stretches between. But it is good. And it is something that makes you better. At listening. At exercising patience. At recognizing that what you have is better than anything you thought could be.

And then, you come to the intersection.

Wet roads. Cars whizzing North. South. And there is a little black-and-white dog. A Shih Tzu. And it is at the other side of the road. Wagging its tail in the rain, the sleet, and looking at you.

"Stay there," I say.

"Oh no, that little dog shouldn't be out in this."

"No," I say. "We'll stop and check for tags."

There is a slight break in traffic.

"What is it, Daddy?" Little Man asks.

"A dog, buddy."

"Why? What is he doing?"

I wait too long. The dog takes a couple steps. Crosses the solid white line of the shoulder and is on the edge of the road.

"Aw shit," I say.

"What? What is he doing?" Little Man shouts.

"Not now," S.B. says to him. "Not now!"

There is a black pickup truck coming from the North. A gray SUV and a red van coming from the South.

The dog takes a few more steps. Wags its tail. Is looking right at us.

"I should have crossed," I say.

The truck rushes by. The dog runs. The gray SUV brakes and brakes and misses. But the red van does not. The dog is hit. S.B. shudders and moans. The kids cry. And the dog flips and bumps along the bottom of the van and comes to rest in the road. I cross the intersection then park far enough away so that S.B. and the kids see as little as possible. The gray SUV has stopped a little ways down the road. The red van has kept going, nearly half a mile away, until it hesitates and finally stops on the side of the road.

I get out and run to the dog.

When I get there, it is clear that there's nothing that can be done. I kneel. The world disappears. And it is just me and this little dog on the middle of US 23 on the cusp of a new year. The sleet has given way to big wet flakes. The cold eases into my hands. My legs. And the dog moves its one good eye to lock onto both of mine. I reach out. Touch her. And she wags her tail. Three times.

I know in my gut what will happen if I lift her up. But there is nothing else I can do. My wife and kids are waiting. The gray SUV is watching. And the red van has made a U-turn and is coming back around.

And so, I pick her up. Cradle her in my arms. And there is the small gurgling sound as her light goes out. And I walk. Away from my family. Away from the road. Through the wet, the snow, and the cold. And even though she has no tags, I know she belongs to someone and I must get her home.